A KILLER'S BARGAIN

A KILLER'S BARGAIN

DEAN OWEN

WILDSIDE PRESS

Published by Wildside Press LLC.
www.wildsidebooks.com

CHAPTER ONE

Rim Bolden knew that this day he would be lucky if he could leave town without using his gun on a man. At the very least it looked as if he would have to fight once, perhaps many times with his fists. And all because men were like they are in a wild place, with nothing to talk about but the war that had ended bitterly for most. Or talk about the market for beef or—talk about women. Mostly the latter, for there were only a few married ones at the lonely ranches around LaVentana, or in the town itself. Of course there were the fancy ones who journeyed up from Paso Del Norte after roundup twice a year. But when it came to single girls a man wanted to marry—Rim Bolden stood tall, his hat off, looking at the stage that had pulled up in front of the LaVentana Hotel in this far corner of the Territory of New Mexico.

The passengers had alighted. The two drummers with sample cases, giving the shabby business block a speculative look as they hurried past staring townspeople.

The driver, holding in the team, peered down at Allie Grindge, who owned the Jewel Saloon and considered himself the official greeter of LaVentana.

"Everybody out, Allie?"

"Soon's I help the lady," Allie Grindge said.

It was the lady that had brought the quick silence to the town. A silence that touched the nerves like the spring winds that howled down from the Mogollons beyond LaVentana. Rim stood awkwardly, knowing that he had faced many things in his twenty-nine years. He had walked from Richmond to Atlanta and beyond with the bullets of Sherman's men seeking him. He had come to New Mexico last year and partnered up with Bert Stallart at Anchor ranch. A small partnership, but one that could bring financial reward to a daring man.

But he knew that facing up to trail dangers all the way to Kansas this spring, would not be nearly as jolting an experience as the one that shaped up now.

Allie Grindge had helped the lady to the walk and the stage pulled out. She looked around, her dusty bonnet tilted on pinned-up pale hair.

Even though she was bundled in a great cloak any man with half an eye could see her condition.

"You're Rim," she said to the tall man in the street who wore his "meeting" clothes; white shirt and black suit, a little shiny from the hard seat of saddle and wagon.

Allie Grindge said, "Welcome to LaVentana."

She pulled away from Grindge and stepped awkwardly from the walk to the street, her skirts trailing dust. "I recognize you from your picture," she said to Rim. "Uncle Bert sent it—"

Rim held his breath, waiting for the first man to speak. Waiting for the first remark, the first laughter. His tall body was like one great steel spring. His hair was black and under it the face that was long and wide at forehead and jaw seemed as pale as that of the female who faced him.

Allie Grindge said from the walk, "Your future bride, Rim." There was a dead silence.

Allie Grindge was not noted for his perceptive powers. Aside from faulty vision which was not improved by steel-rimmed spectacles, his wit was lacking. And they said it would take a twenty-pound sledge to drive anything into his head.

Rim stood rigid. "Hello, Ellamae. I—I've got the wagon here."

He took her arm, wishing he had worn his belt gun. He looked carefully at each man who sat stiffly on the loafer's benches, or those who had come out of their stores to witness the arrival of the stage. Even five minutes ago they had been joshing Rim, asking him when the wedding would be. For the arrival of anyone as young and pretty as Ellamae Stallart was an occasion in this lonely place. And Bert Stallart, Rim's partner at Anchor, had more than once passed his niece's photograph around for all to see and admire. It was Stallart who had first braced Rim about "keeping Anchor in the family." Rim should marry Ellamae when she came out from Joplin. How could a man do better? And Rim agreed that it was a tempting idea, but he pointed out to him marriage was something serious. A man married a woman because he loved her. Not just because she was niece to his partner and marriage to her would assure a larger financial interest in a potentially great ranch.

Rim watched the stony faces. He thought he saw amusement on some, but it was not open. No smiles, no digging elbows in ribs. Just silence.

It felt to him as if the very street upon which he stood was shifting. No foundation at all under the built-up heels of his town boots but quicksand. Through his mind spun the things Stallart had said, "If you do get married," Stallart had told him, "it'll take away some of the talk about you and Marcy." Marcy was Stallart's handsome dark-haired wife. It was the first time Rim had felt like hitting his partner in the face.

Rim Bolden walked Ellamae to the Anchor wagon. "Can you make it?" he said. "I mean can you climb to the seat by yourself?"

She nodded and he got behind her and steadied her foot on the step. He pushed and got her up to the seat.

He went around to the other side, his face ashen.

"Looks like you'll have to be a mite quick with the preacher, Rim," a voice cut out from the doorway of the Jewel Saloon. "She's liable to drop her foal before you can get a ring on her finger."

Rim turned slowly, conscious that the silence along the street had thickened even more. In the distance he could see the balloon of dust from the departing stage. He could hear a dog's snarl of displeasure in the alley behind the saloon.

Rim said over his shoulder to a man standing by a fire barrel. "Will you hold the team so they won't run?"

"Sure, Rim. Sure—"

A window banged up above the Jewel Saloon. A plump, powdered face, topped by a red wig was thrust out.

"Don't have no trouble now," the woman's harsh voice shouted. "That poor gal's sufferin' enough as it is. Bolden, you better think twice about taking her all the way out to Anchor in a wagon. The jolting won't do her no good at all."

Rim looked at the upstairs window. "Daisy, maybe you could come down and give me a hand with her. And maybe one of you boys can get hold of Doc Snider."

"Doc's gone down to Mesilla."

Rim clenched his teeth and for the first time looked directly at the man who had made the insulting remark about Ellamae dropping her foal.

The man was Rim's height, six feet. He wore a brown wool shirt and brown pants and half boots. Around his waist was slung a .45 in a silver-studded rig. He had light blue eyes and hair nearly the shade of Ellamae's. His ranch bordered on Anchor at the foot of the Mogollons near one of the forks of the Gila River. His name was Eric Ward. He had come here just before Christmas when the snow was deep. A poor time for a man to start ranching everybody said.

"Bolden, don't let Ward push you into something," Daisy yelled from the second-floor window. "That poor gal can't stand to get all upset."

Rim took a deep breath and turned his back on Ward. If possible, he wanted to get Stallart's niece out of town. Then he could settle other things.

Rim started to take the reins from the man who was holding them. He heard a step behind him.

Ward said, "Stallart should give you a half interest in Anchor for doing this job, Bolden."

Rim turned. "What job?" he asked quietly.

"Saving him from the disgrace of a niece who—"

"That's enough, Ward!"

"You'll marry her, won't you?" Ward pressed on, his handsome face smiling. It seemed to Rim that Eric Ward was making an unnecessary point in all this. But the reason escaped him.

The crowd had moved up, the more venturesome. Others were hurrying into stores, taking refuge behind walls of 'dobe or brick.

"You do whatever Stallart tells you," Ward said. "You'll marry his pregnant niece—you'll use a running iron on your neighbor's beef."

Rim had been watching Ward's right hand. It started downward, fingers seeking the walnut grips of his .45. Rim closed in, got both hands on the strong wrist. He swung Ward around, tore free the gun and threw it into the street. The shouting caused horses to rear, and another man sprang forward to help hold the Anchor team.

Upstairs Daisy shouted shrilly, "Quit it. That poor kid is—" Her voice was drowned out.

Hanging onto the right arm, Rim used his body as a pivot. He spun Ward, sent him crashing into the fire barrel at the edge of the walk. The rotted slats gave way under the weight of Ward's body. For an instant he seemed suspended by a shelf of slimy water. Then the water roared out and Ward fell into the wreckage.

Ward managed to get his elbows under him. "You gutless swine!" he cried. "You're not man enough to come for me with a gun!"

"Next time I'll wear one," Rim said.

"Next time you'll need one!" Drenched, Ward stood there angrily. Bits of cigarette paper clung to his clothing for the fire barrel was used as a repository for many things in LaVentana. Mostly it was known as a community spitoon.

Rim walked over to the wagon and jerked free his rifle from under the seat. He levered in a shell, faced Ward. "You've called me a thief. You've insulted a woman—"

"She insulted herself, by doing what she did with some man."

"After this, keep out of my way," Rim warned.

"I might give you the same advice. Particularly where it applies to my range. I have a fondness for my own beef. I don't care to see my T brand end up as an Anchor Bar."

Rim said, "It might be interesting to find out why you took a brand that could be so easily altered."

"I don't have to answer questions from a man who was traitor to his country."

Rim looked at him. "I thought that question was settled when Lee gave up his sword."

"It'll never be settled in my mind." Ward looked around. "In *our* minds."

Nobody spoke up in defense of Ward's ideas. But Rim noticed a few cautious nods of agreement.

He drove Ellamae out of town. The road to Anchor was rough and he tried to keep the team to a walk, but they were frisky and had not been run for nearly a week. He thought of how he had picked this spirited team, thinking it would give a girl like Ellamae a thrill to ride out to Anchor in fine style. But now—

Ellamae said, "I didn't think it would be like this. They said the stage would get in after dark. I—I didn't think anybody would see me."

"You can't depend on a stage schedule in these parts. I've been in town all day waiting for you."

"It's a disappointment, isn't it, Rim?"

"Call it surprise."

"I—I wanted to write Uncle Bert, but—Uncle Bert's wife, Aunt Marcy, wrote me such a nice letter and said I was always welcome. I thought that on a ranch I could—could have my baby without too many people knowing about it."

"I don't suppose it would do any good to ask who the man was."

"I—I loved this one more than the others. Really. We were going to get married, but he—died." She put a hand to her eyes. "I just hope I can make it up to Uncle Bert. Aunt Marcy wrote that he's the most generous man she ever knew."

Rim said nothing. He was thinking that more than one man said that Bert Stallart, once he was aroused, had the most explosive temper north of Ciudad Chihuahua.

One thing constructive had been accomplished this day at least. The undercover bitterness between Anchor Bar and Eric Ward's T ranch had at last come into the open. As he drove, the New Mexico dust stinging his eyes, he thought of what Ward had said. He had called Rim Bolden a thief, in so many words. He said that Rim Bolden took Stallart's orders. Whether it was using a running iron on a neighbor's beef. Or marrying a pregnant niece—

Rim glanced at the girl riding so stiff on the seat at his side. He tried not to look at her swollen body, but how could you help it? He thought back to the meeting at the stage. How he had removed his hat and waited like some actor on a stage for her arrival. Ready for the joshing of the townspeople. Accepting it before the stage arrived, knowing it would be intensified once the girl was on his arm. Because those people would have a method in their teasing. A wedding was an excuse to put aside the work and remember that there were other things in life beside the constant fight for survival in a hard land.

Because there seemed to be an endless stream of men moving west; those of Eric Ward's breed. Men dedicated to the taking of property that belonged to another. From the first day Ward appeared, after taking over the old 25 ranch, Rim had warned Stallart. But Bert Stallart said no man was fool enough to tangle with Anchor.

Rim had the feeling that Stallart's ideas had lately undergone a change. It was certain that Stallart and Marcy weren't getting along. Rim had heard Marcy sobbing of a night.

One day Rim had asked Marcy about this change in her husband. But Marcy gave a hopeless shake of her head and said she didn't know. But maybe when Ellamae came to stay with them it might cheer up Bert Stallart—

"I feel horrid," Ellamae said, and groaned. "That stage like to tore me apart it jolted so."

The road climbed through pines and in the distance could be seen the shimmering green of aspens. Far below the road a stream flashed its silvered frothy way down a canyon.

They came at last within sight of Anchor headquarters, a collection of frame and log buildings on a great knoll of cleared land.

Rim sensed the girl's growing tension.

"I brought a present," she said, and from a pocket of her cloak, produced an orange. It was bright in color and she seemed proud of it. She said it had come upriver from New Orleans and before that from Seville.

But Rim doubted the fruit could stay fresh that long. "A real orange," he said, and tried to sound pleased.

"Will Uncle Bert and Aunt Marcy like it?"

"I shouldn't wonder."

He had a feeling. It was like the planned retreat of the war. Strategy, they said. You retreated and your belly turned sour and you shared your dead horse with your men. You found your boots worn through and your feet bleeding. You tried to fight, but how do you fight an avalanche? They were pressing on, the great bayoneted wave of blue. He had the same feeling today, as he saw the wisps of smoke curling from the stone chimneys of the main house.

Disaster pressing in on you.

He slowed the team. When Marcy suggested she and Stallart accompany Rim to town to meet Ellamae, Stallart had shaken his head, grinning. "Leave the young folks have the ride out from town to get acquainted."

Now Rim could feel perspiration at the edge of his dark hair. It glistened on the high cheekbones, salted the corners of his wide mouth. As he was thinking, a man makes plans and counts on the second half of his life being better than the first. He puts down his roots with a partner he trusts. And then a girl looks too long at the moon one night in Joplin—

CHAPTER TWO

With a steadying hand on her arm Rim Bolden escorted Stallart's niece along a narrow hallway, past the door to the kitchen where pots steamed on a big stove. Then into the vast parlor with its stone fireplace, the logs flaming. Indian rugs brightened the floor. There were leather sofas and chairs made of hardwood with a latticework of wide leathers for the seat.

The big room was empty, but Rim could hear someone walking around upstairs.

"Company's here," he called out, in what he hoped was a strong clear voice.

There were muted exclamations and the sound of hurrying steps. Rim pushed Ellamae down into one of the leather sofas where Marcy's large sewing basket had been set. Ellamae picked up the basket and held it in her lap and looked frightened as a burly man hurried down.

"Ellamae!" Stallart shouted, big hand outstretched. He laughed. "What you doing with Marcy's sewing basket? By God, Rim, you teaching her how to keep house already?"

Stallart seized his niece's hand, pumped it.

From a corner of his eye Rim saw Marcy halt abruptly on the landing. Marcy's dark head was inclined as she stared at Ellamae sitting on the sofa. And the dark eyes mirrored shock and consternation. And then a swift pity. He saw the handsome face of Stallart's wife go pale around the full mouth. She wore a bright dress of green silk that Rim knew she had brought with her from Natchez.

"Welcome, Ellamae," Marcy said in her deeply pleasant voice. As she crossed the room her gaze touched Rim's. And there was a deepening fear in her eyes, a silent plea for help.

Stallart said, "Marcy, she's got the Stallart look. She have any youn-guns and they'll favor the Stallart side." He turned to Rim. "Might be you won't like that." He gave Rim a broad man-to-man wink.

Rim said nothing. It was a long time since he'd seen his partner in such a jovial mood. This was the old Bert Stallart, the one he had first known and liked. Not the sullen, suspicious whisky drinker he had become lately.

"You're a mite plump," Stallart said appraisingly. "But then a gal with meat on her bones is fine for this country." The man-to-man wink again. "We have some cold winters hereabouts, huh, Rim."

Rim looked sick.

Stallart noticed the silence of his wife and partner, the obvious fright of his niece. He looked perplexed.

There was about Stallart something of the grizzly bear. He had wild, shaggy hair, so thick you'd break the teeth of the ordinary comb just trying to get the tangles out. His face was broad, weathered, red when he was angered. He had a large nose, dipped slightly where the hard heel of a cowman's boot had struck during a forgotten brawl. He wore a shirt of rough wool, tight across his big shoulders. The shirt was also tight at the belly where he was beginning to show his forty-five years.

"You act like it's a funeral instead of a welcome," Stallart said. "Damn it, I'm going to have a drink. A little sherry, Ellamae? Or maybe you ain't never done anything so sinful as take a drink." Without giving her a chance to reply he moved ponderously to a sideboard that Marcy kept polished. It had come to New Mexico with her in the wagon. Her parents were buried at Paso where they were taken with the plague.

The muscles in Marcy's pale throat seemed to stiffen. "Bert, I think I heard one of the men calling you. Jellick, I think."

"What the hell's that hoss breaker want with me? Let him stew! By God, this is the same as Christmas and Appomattox Day all rolled into one. Beggin' your pardon, Rim," he added quickly. "Reckon it wasn't much of a holiday for you fellas."

"I think I'll go out and look over that new string Jellick is breaking," Rim said. "Glad to have met you, Miss Stallart."

"Miss Stallart!" Bert Stallart boomed. "The hell with that. It's Ellamae." He came across the room, the floor planks squealing under his weight. He handed a glass of sherry to Ellamae and one to the pale Marcy. "You need more color, Marcy," he told his wife. "You don't get outside enough. Now that Ellamae's here you and her can go to town and—" Stallart looked around at the three solemn faces. "What's goin' on!" he demanded, and Rim could see the angry color move slowly up under Stallart's coarse skin.

Rim said, "I really ought to go, Bert. After all, this is a family re-union—"

"You stay." Stallart squinted at Ellamae. "I begin to savvy now. You kids had a few words, huh?" He grinned. "Well, you got to remember, Rim, a woman travels a long ways setting on the hard seat of a coach and it shortens her temper. A gentle girl like Ellamae ain't used to things like that."

Marcy was twisting her hands together and Rim could see that her knuckles were startlingly white. Ellamae clung to the sewing basket on her lap.

Marcy said, "Bert, you and Rim go out and look—look at those horses Jellick is breaking."

"Get some food on the table and quit worrying about hosses," Stallart said, and gave his wife a good-natured slap on the back. Turning, he grabbed Ellamae's hand. "Stand up, gal, let me look at you." He jerked Ellamae to her feet in his rough way, and the sewing basket spilled its socks and rolled across the floor to the edge of a thick wool rug. "This is the house for a wedding," Stallart went on in his booming way. By God, we'll have everybody for a hundred miles. We'll send invites clear down to Mesilla—"

Stallart's voice broke off and the quick amber gaze roved over the length of Ellamae's swollen body. She stood with one hand helplessly at her side, the other gripped in her uncle's fist. At first Stallart looked puzzled, then pained. He shot Marcy a glance, as if saying, What does it mean? Does it mean what I think?

Marcy stood with her hands clasped before her green dress, the knuckles pressed against her breasts. Her head was bowed. Rim could see the clean white part in her hair and he felt a surge of pity. He wanted to put out a hand and draw her against him and let her weep and feel her warm wet tears—

The rage in Stallart's heavy face was marked by a vivid red. There was a hard line of mouth beneath the thick, tobacco-stained downsweeping mustache.

Rim took the orange Ellamae had given him, from his pocket. "This is a present," he said. "For all we know, it might have come all the way from Spain."

Marcy's dark eyes flashed Rim a look of gratitude for this interruption. "Peel it carefully, Rim," she said, and her voice shook a little. Then, with her shoulders back she stepped up to Ellamae and put a hand on the arm of the girl. "We are glad you came to stay with us, Ellamae—"

A spate of tears gushed suddenly from Ellamae's eyes. She flung wide her cloak. "Take a good look. Now you know why I wanted to visit with you!"

Marcy closed the cloak. "It's all right, dear." She put a hand against Ellamae's forehead. "I wish you would have explained. I would have met you in town. We should get the doctor—" She looked at her husband, who stood rigid, unspeaking. Then to the girl, Marcy went on, "The wagon must have been agony for you. It's so near your—time."

Ellamae's mouth jerked and a hard bright gleam touched her eyes. "Uncle Bert doesn't want me here!"

"Yes, he does, dear."

"My being here will bring you nothing but trouble. In town Rim hit a man who made an insulting remark—"

Stallart said, "Who was it, Rim?" And when Rim told him Eric Ward, Stallart said, "I'll apologize to Ward for what you done, Rim."

Rim, peeling the orange, said, "It was my fight, Bert. You better leave it lay."

"You don't need to fight for this wanton no more," Stallart said, jerking a thumb at his niece.

Ellamae squealed as if lashed across the face with a rope end, and Marcy said, "You shouldn't talk like that, Bert. She's your kin."

Stallart made a cutting motion with his hand. "No kin of mine. My brother Paul was her pa and—" Stallart's voice trailed away. And Rim watched him, remembering that Stallart always got a haunted look whenever he mentioned his brother. The brother was dead and Ellamae's mother had died at her birth and Rim knew that some woman in Joplin had raised the girl. The woman had recently died.

"Leave the girl alone, Bert," Rim advised, and put the peelings of the orange on the table. "She's been through enough already."

Stallart's gaze was hot "Rim, I ain't known a man who was more a brother to me than you. A son almost. But by God you tell me my business and you can ride."

Marcy looked stunned. "Bert, you didn't mean that."

Stallart gave his wife an ugly smile. "What's the matter? You got a *reason* for wanting him to stay?"

Marcy, her face white, said, "Rim, I haven't tasted an orange since I was a little girl." She held out a hand. Rim could see that it shook slightly.

Rim finished peeling it and some of the precious juice ran over the tips of his fingers and onto the floor. In the stillness of the big room he could hear the murmur of voices from the yard as the crew had their evening smoke. It was getting dark in the house. He halved the orange, then quartered it. He stripped the slices and held them out to Marcy.

She took two of them and handed one to Ellamae. But the girl turned her head. She was biting her lip so hard Rim could see a dot of blood on her chin.

Marcy said, "You best go upstairs and lie down."

She started to lead Ellamae toward the stairs, but the girl wavered. Rim dropped the orange slices to the table and sprang to catch her before her head struck the floor. He carried her up the stairs, aware that Stallart's burning gaze was on the back of his head.

In the spare bedroom Rim put the girl down on a serape that covered the bed. Ellamae was moaning, her eyes tightly closed.

A lock of Marcy's dark hair had fallen across her face. "I only hope Bert doesn't take to the bottle tonight. He's done it so much lately."

"If he does, call me," Rim said.

She tried to smile. Then she turned quickly to the bed as Ellamae gave a sharp cry. "Rim, could you send one of the men for Doc Snider?"

Rim told her that he'd heard in town the doctor was visiting in Mesilla.

"It means he'll probably be gone a month," Marcy said helplessly. "Whisky and that Sanchez woman. But then I guess you can't blame him too much, living in a place like LaVentana."

"Is there anything I can do?" Rim asked, looking at Ellamae who was beginning to writhe on the bed.

Marcy said, "If necessary I can do it alone." Then a bitterness came to her eyes. "I used to watch Tessa, my mammy, when one of the slaves had a child—Oh, yes, Rim. I come from a very proud family. Just like the Stallarts. Without sin. But we did own human beings as you would own a horse or a gun or a pair of boots." She swallowed and turned her head. "When you go downstairs, try and talk sense to Bert."

Rim nodded. He went out, closing the door, shutting off the sounds of grinding pain that burst from Ellamae's lips with increasing frequency.

Rim saw that Stallart was staring at the orange slices on the table. Stallart looked around, stricken. "Sorry I blowed the powder at you, Rim, but—"

"She was going to get married, Bert. Her intended was killed—"

Rim was instantly sorry he had spoken, for it touched the raw nerve that rekindled Stallart's rage. "Ain't no excuse," Stallart cried, "for a woman laying with a man 'less she's got a ring on her finger!"

"Might be a good thing," Rim said, looking Stallart in the eye, "if *everybody* remembered that the next time the fancy women come up from Paso."

A quick shame touched Stallart's eyes, then turned to belligerence. "With a man it's different."

Rim felt his anger slowly rising and he wanted to fight it. He wanted to forget the humiliation in town today when one minute he had been joshed about his possible marriage to the new visitor from Joplin. And the next minute seeing her obviously pregnant.

"Goddam it, Bert," Rim said with cold emphasis, "we've got the cow business to worry about. Forget about Ellamae. She's your dead brother's girl, no matter what she's done."

Rim snatched two of the precious orange slices from the table and went out into the darkness. He crossed the yard. Lights bloomed yellowly in the bunkhouse windows. There was in the air the smell of manure and horse sweat and the odors of men who worked hard and long. The cherry red ends of their cigarettes glowed in the evening shadows.

The men were strangely silent tonight, Rim noticed, as he angled for his quarters built on one end of the bunkhouse. Nobody said, "Hi, Rim," or "I feel lucky tonight. How about gettin 'even with you?" Rim was a partner-foreman and he believed while working that there should be a gulf of sorts between himself and his men. But when evening came it was different.

He knew their silence tonight stemmed from the presence of Stallart's niece. The word would have been swiftly passed by those who saw her arrive in the wagon.

And at that moment came a tight scream from the second floor of the house. Rim halted, looked back at the house. Then he started on again.

By the bunkhouse wall Meade Jellick, the big horse breaker, was sitting on his heels, casting a giant shadow.

When the scream was repeated, Jellick said, "Somebody step on a cat's tail?" One of the men snickered.

Rim kept on walking toward his quarters. But he slanted a glance at Jellick that warned the man to keep his mouth shut. He didn't care much for Jellick.

"She's a good-looker," Jellick said, and Rim halted, seeing the shine of Jellick's big teeth in the darkness. In a country of big men Jellick bragged that he was the biggest. And he was, so far as Rim had seen.

Jellick laughed quietly, "Wish I'd been the one to make her big around the middle."

"Pack your gear, Jellick," Rim said crisply. "Then step into my office for your time."

Jellick got up. "You ain't got the brains of a jack-legged hoss, Bolden. You steaming up a storm on account of I said I'd like to have been the one to pester that good-lookin' yellow-haired gal—"

"Jellick, get off this property!"

"—when everybody knows you been usin' the boss' wife for a saddle."

Rim froze. He heard a collective gasp from the men. Saw some of them move quickly away from Jellick.

"You was lucky with Ward in town today. You won't be so lucky with me." Jellick clenched his fists.

"How do you know what happened in town today?"

There was amusement in Jellick's tone when he said, "Ain't all of us here drawing only Anchor pay." He hitched up his pants. "I ain't wearing a gun, Bolden. It'll be fists, huh?" He laughed. "Right here and now!"

CHAPTER THREE

Rim started for Jellick. But a voice from the cookhouse doorway across the yard, said sharply, "Hold it, Jellick!"

Ed Rule, the Anchor cook, gray tufts of hair jutting from his skull, was holding a shotgun. "You heard the boss, Jellick. Get out!" And then the old man swung his gaze to Rim. "I'm sorry, Rim. But dammit in the dark like this you wouldn't have no chance with him."

"I think maybe I would," Rim said coldly.

"No, Rim. Damn it. He'd put his bootheels through your face before you'd know which end of the bottle to pour from."

Without taking his eyes from the giant Jellick, Rim said, "Put down the shotgun, Ed. I mean it!"

"You'll have to take it away from me, Rim."

Jellick went into the bunkhouse and after a minute came out with his warsack. He walked on down to the nearest rail where a big Morgan was tied. He swung lightly into the saddle.

"You wasted breath firing me, Bolden," Jellick said. "I already quit. I'm working for T. Ward's outfit. See you, *neighbor!*"

Laughing, he rode off into the darkness.

For a long moment Rim stood there, his muscles rigid. Gradually his breathing returned to normal. Ed Rule had put up the shotgun.

"Believe, me, Rim," the cook said across the yard. "He'd have kicked your head loose. I seen him kill a man in a brawl at Denver."

"Ed, you're an old man. There aren't many jobs for a man your age. Don't step on my command again. I run this outfit, you don't."

Rim walked over to where the twenty-odd Anchor men were a silent group in front of the bunkhouse.

"Who was in town today?" Rim asked. And when none of them answered, Rim said, "I want the name of the man who was in town."

At last Tut Tyler said, "It was me, Rim."

"You brought out the news that I'd tangled with Eric Ward today."

"Well, Ward asked me to tell Jellick about it and—"

Rim looked around, and said, "How many of you boys are taking money from Ward?"

Nobody said anything, but Tyler. "I ain't drawin' pay, it's just that Ward asked me a favor."

"You're through here, Tyler."

Rim walked over to the cook shack. Ed Rule sat at the big plank table where the men took their meals. He was drinking coffee, pouring in molasses for a sweetener.

"Didn't mean to bark at you, Ed," Rim said. "But we're in for trouble. Ward is starting to get itchy. This business of Stallart's niece isn't going to help any."

"Yeah. I just couldn't stand still and listen to Jellick talk about Marcy Stallart. I wanted to use that shotgun on him."

"I'll handle him in my own time, Ed." Rim frowned. "I have a feeling about Jellick. Have had ever since Bert hired him on."

Rim broke off, for Bert Stallart entered the cookhouse. His eyes were already getting as red as his face. Rim could smell whisky on his breath. "I heard an argument a minute ago," Stallart said. "What's the trouble?"

"I just fired Meade Jellick."

"You *what!*"

Rim Bolden waited for the burst of wrath he expected from Stallart, because he could see the hard amber gaze. But then Stallart put a shaking hand across his mouth as if to press flat the mustache. "You should've talked it over with me first," he said shakily. "Jellick is a sort of special hand. He—he—well, we need a good hoss breaker."

"There are others."

"But you don't understand."

"Jellick insulted a woman," Rim said, and hoped he didn't have to go into details.

At that moment Marcy Stallart called her husband from the upstairs window. Stallart was wanted, right away.

Stallart made as if to ignore her, then shrugged and plodded across the yard.

When Rim was alone again with the cook, he said, "What's so special about Meade Jellick?"

"I heard Jellick say once that he knowed Bert back in Kansas."

Rim frowned, wondering why Stallart had never said anything about it to him. It was a month since Jellick had been hired on. That day Rim was in LaVentana and when he returned Stallart said he had hired somebody to build up a remuda for roundup. He said that Meade Jellick was a drifter. Jellick could ride, Rim had to admit. But Rim was against hiring a man of Jellick's size. A good horse could be ruined making his first sunfish with two hundred and forty pounds on his back.

"Bert mention anything else about Jellick?" Rim asked.

Ed Rule seemed to be making quite a project of hanging a few battered pans on wall hooks above his stove. "Well, not exactly," Rule said slowly.

"How do you mean that, Ed?"

"I was here in the cookshack one day and Jellick and Stallart was right outside the window yonder when Marcy came outa the house to water her garden. And I heard Jellick say kind of soft-like, 'Mrs. Stallart sure looks good. I'd like to see her after she's been in a rainstorm with her clothes all hangin' tight against her!'"

Rim was aware of a small pulse at his temple. "You're sure Jellick said that?"

"As near as I can remember, that's what he said. There wasn't no wondering about what he meant."

"And what did Stallart do?"

Ed Rule looked grim. "He never said one damn word."

"I never knew Bert Stallart to back down from an insult. I sure as hell can't figure him letting a man say a thing like that about his wife."

"Any other man but Jellick," Ed Rule said quietly, "would have been dead. Rim, you better buy yourself an extra eye to stick between your shoulder blades. That Jellick is the kind to do his shooting from the brush. After tonight he ain't going to feel kindly toward you."

Rim went down to his quarters. It was a twelve by twelve room, big enough for a bunk, desk, a couple of chairs and a big iron safe. He sank into a chair and put his bootheels on a spur-scarred desk. There was a knock at the door and Rim told whoever it was to come in.

It was Willie Temple, Marcy's brother. He was slim and dark and had his sister's good looks. "You look pretty sad, Rim. I hear you and Jellick sawed your tempers up short."

"Where were you when it happened?" Rim asked sharply, wondering if Willie had heard the reason for the trouble—Marcy.

Willie Temple said he had been down to the horse camp by the river where he'd been helping repair a corral. Willie Temple was a segundo of sorts. He was a willing worker if you leaned on him a little. But he'd rather play poker or tip a bottle than work. Rim liked him well enough, but considered him a liability. Because Willie was Marcy's brother and Stallart's brother-in-law, he got special consideration. He made fifty dollars a month, which was twice what some of the hands were getting. Rim felt he had never earned it. But he and Willie hit it off when there wasn't work to be done.

Rim had put the two orange slices in his shirt pocket when Jellick started his loud talk. He removed them from his pocket. "Saved a slice for you, Willie."

"A real orange," Willie Temple said, impressed.

They sat quietly in the small room and made a ceremony out of eating the two slices.

"Sour," Rim said.

"You're wrong. It's the sweetest thing I ever tasted," Willie said.

The eating of the orange consumed much time. First Rim nibbled at an end. He would let a little of the juice trickle into his mouth. Then he would carefully chew the pulp, extracting every last bit of flavor.

"I remember one Christmas," Willie said, "when they had orange slices tied to a tree at the Yardly Store in Natchez. I was just a kid. I always wanted to taste an orange. Now I have."

"Me too," Rim said, and gave Willie a tight grin. There was nearly ten years difference in their ages.

"Too bad you weren't around then, Rim," Willie said darkly. "About the time I saw the orange in Yardly's Store. Marcy was a pretty little thing then."

"She still is."

Willie nodded. "But she won't be long. I wish you had been the one to marry her."

"There's already too much talk about Marcy," Rim snapped. "And about me."

"Well, it's no secret she likes you."

"Sure. And I like her. As Bert Stallart's wife."

Willie Temple got up, smiling. "I wish I had you for a brother-in-law instead of—Well, forget it. Thanks for the orange."

As Willie started for the door Rim blocked it. Willie was shorter, fifty pounds lighter. "We've got a good thing here, Willie. Let's not any of us ruin it."

"Oh, hell, Rim—"

"You're segundo. A pretty responsible job." And Rim thought, If you only worked at it. "It's better than forking hay at the livery in town."

Rim tried to say it lightly and with a small laugh. To show Willie that he was only joking, but to impress upon Willie that for a young man he had come far by being Stallart's brother-in-law. A long way from the impoverished plantation where he had been born.

But Willie's good-looking face darkened. "I didn't need Bert Stallart tying up with my sister to pull me out of that job."

The door suddenly banged open and Bert Stallart walked in. He was bareheaded. The wind must have come up because his long stringy hair was loose about his face. His eyes were getting that mean-hoss look, and the odor of whisky was so strong that a man might wonder if he rinsed his shirt in the stuff.

"What the hell's the matter with you?" Stallart demanded, staring at his brother-in-law's angry face.

But Willie didn't even bother to reply. He stomped out, slamming the door behind him.

"He turns my stomach like a drink of warm tequila," Stallart said. "What ails him."

"He's young, full of fire." Rim tried to smile. He was a little irritated that Stallart always walked in without knocking.

Stallart seemed to forget about Willie Temple. He whipped around a chair and straddled it. "It's a boy, Rim. By God, it's a boy!"

For a moment Rim didn't comprehend; so much had happened this day. "You mean that Ellamae—" Rim was relieved that Stallart was so joyous. "She gave birth to a boy?"

"He ain't much bigger'n the crown of my hat. You know what?" Stallart dug a half-filled whisky bottle from his pocket. He passed it to Rim, who took a small drink, then handed it back.

Stallart almost killed the bottle. "I got me an idea, Rim. See what you think of it. Maybe you didn't know it but Marcy can't have no kids. Some accident when she was a kid. Wagon rolled over on her—Anyhow, it was some disappointment when I heard it. A man counts on raising a family."

"Sure, Bert. What's this about Ellamae's boy?"

"It ain't her boy, Rim," he said, the lips under the down-sweeping mustache suddenly taut. "I'll raise the boy as my own. What do you think of it, Rim?"

"I think it's just about the whitest thing a man could do. But—"

"But what? Goddam it, speak up."

"Does Ellamae want to give him up?"

"What the hell's *she* got to do with it? Stallart ran a tongue looking like a piece of dyed red leather over his mustache. He finished the bottle, threw it on Rim's cot. "I always sort of figured you for my son, Rim. Even if I'm only fifteen or so years older. But now—"

"You'll have a real son." Rim wondered how Ellamae would take this. "It'll be a great thing for Marcy. Having the boy around to raise."

But Stallart seemed only interested in the boy. As he formulated his plans his speech began to thicken as the whisky took hold. He would send the boy East to school. And when he was grown he would run Anchor. "Of course you'll still be a partner and ramrod as long as you live, Rim."

Rim felt uncomfortable. It was almost as if Stallart was saying in so many words that he didn't expect Rim Bolden to live long enough to interfere with any plans this new son might have upon reaching his majority.

Stallart made his stumbling way to the door. He turned to look back at Rim. Suddenly the exuberance at the birth of this boy faded from his eyes. They were hard.

"Just happened to think of something, Rim. When I ain't to home, maybe it'd be better if you didn't go up to the house no more."

Rim got slowly to his feet. "I've never been in that house when you're not home."

"Well, I heard different, but it don't make no mind. I just figured it looks better. You know how some folks talk."

Rim came up to him. "It does too make some mind, Bert."

"It's why I was hoping you'd hitch up with Ellamae. With a wife of your own there wouldn't be no talk. You see how it is. But I know you wouldn't marry a wanton like Ellamae—"

"But you do think I should have a wife."

"A man can wear his socks to bed or he can put his cold feet on a woman's leg. I'd rather it was the leg, if it was me."

"Bert, I'd like to go over some things we've got to face."

"Ain't nothing that won't wait till morning."

"Somebody's trying awfully damned hard to drive an ax between us, Bert. I've got a feeling that Eric Ward is behind it."

Stallart's eyes were guarded. "How you figure?"

"Jellick said he was going to work for Ward and—"

Stallart flinched. "Jellick wouldn't do that. He couldn't—" Stallart looked sick.

"You and Meade Jellick are old friends?"

"Never seen him before in my life till I hired him on," Stallart said with more vehemence than the remark warranted.

"Oh. I'd heard you knew each other back in Kansas."

"Now who the hell would spread a lie like that?" Stallart stood rigid; the alcohol that had shrouded his eyes seemed gone. His gaze was bright, intent. When Rim didn't say anything Stallart opened the door, letting in the sharp mountain cold. "You come up for breakfast like usual, Rim."

"I think I'd better eat with the men after this."

"I never meant anything, Rim. Jeez, let Marcy cook for you like she always does—" Stallart ran a shaking hand over his face. "Don't get your back bowed up like a mule with a pole at his rump. I just meant that when I ain't to home you and Marcy—" He gave a feeble grin. "I'm going back to the house and see how my boy is getting along."

Rim listened to his fading footsteps in the yard. One thing was clear to him now. His stay at Anchor would be much shorter than he intended.

CHAPTER FOUR

Eric Ward was in the yard of T Ranch, gripping a rifle when Jellick appeared as a giant shadow out of the deeper darkness of the night. There was likely no man in this corner of New Mexico or in the whole territory, for that matter, who would throw as large a shadow as Jellick.

Ward stepped away from the stand of aspens where he had waited since he first heard the labored plod of a horse making the climb to the shelf of land where Ward had his headquarters. "You have some news?" Ward asked.

"You think I rode all the way over here just so you could ask me that?"

"Don't get smart. I suppose the niece has gladdened Stallart's heart by now," Ward said with a laugh.

"Tut Tyler said you saw her in town. She's big as a barrel of Weigand's Beer. Must be triplets."

"How did Stallart take it?"

"Not too good, from the yelling that went on in the house. I didn't get a chance to stay around. Me and your friend Rim Bolden—"

"I hope you jumped on his head."

"I wanted to, but he fired me."

"You told him where you stand? With me?"

"I told him," Jellick said. "That cook Rule put a gun at my back. I didn't figure to buck that. Anyhow, what's the hurry? So Bolden lives the week out. What's the difference?"

Ward scowled and put a hand to a bruise on his left shoulder suffered in the skirmish with Rim Bolden in town. "Just so he's dead is all that matters to me, I thought I had the job finished today in LaVentana, but he was lucky—"

Jellick stomped in his boots to settle his feet. "Tyler says Bolden knocked hell out of you in town," Jellick drawled, and Ward sensed the man was smiling. But Jellick stood in such deep shadow that he couldn't be sure. It was really just an impression rather than anything he could see. Jellick went on, "But then I don't believe half of what Tyler says. And then only if he's got one hand on the Bible."

"Bolden and I did have some trouble," Ward admitted gruffly. But he didn't go into details.

"Tyler got fired," Jellick said. "He caught up with me. Said Bolden got tough after I left and wanted to know who else was on your payroll at Anchor."

Ward peered down the steep trail where trees grew thickly and made the night even blacker. "Didn't Tyler come with you?"

"He went to town. Said he'd be out tomorrow. I got the feeling he's goin' to miss the boys at Anchor."

"The trouble with Tyler," Ward said, "is that he's got nothing on his mind but that Daisy."

"My hoss is better lookin' front and back than her."

Ward went inside his house. Jellick unsaddled and joined him. The house was small. It once had belonged to a cowman named Grimes who tried to run beef here when the Apaches still considered this their private hunting preserve. His cows didn't last long and neither did he. The Apaches had fired the house, but only a part of the roof burned off. Probably the rest of the house was saved by one of the thundershowers so frequent here at certain times of the year. At least that was the way Ward figured it. After he paid Grimes' widow, who was living in Mesilla, four bits an acre for the land, he put on a new roof and had the place cleaned up, and the existing corral repaired and a new one built west of the house.

"Stallart's niece showing up like this," Jellick said, helping himself to a bottle Ward had put on the table, "sort of changes our plans."

"Well, she won't be Rim Bolden's widow," Ward said. "It's for certain he won't marry her under existing circumstances. Not unless he's a damn fool. And this I doubt very much."

"He's damn fool enough to mess with Stallart's wife."

"That's the part I don't like!"

"It was your idea," Jellick said, tossing off a drink of Ward's whisky. "You left a note or two where Stallart could find 'em and—"

"I know that," Ward said impatiently. "I hadn't met Mrs. Stallart then. I didn't realize the kind of woman she is."

"Well, they're messin' together. Her and Bolden."

Ward, pouring himself a drink, eyed the big man who overflowed a chair on the other side of the table. The chair had wired-up rungs. "Is this something you know for a fact?" Ward said sharply.

"You can tell how things is between 'em. By the way they're always lookin' at each other."

"But you don't really *know.*"

Jellick's broad face flushed in the lamp glow. "What difference does it make? Stallart's beginning to watch 'em. That's the main thing."

"Just how did you plant suspicion in Stallart's mind?" Ward asked, knowing this wouldn't be too difficult an accomplishment when you took into consideration some of the tragic events in Stallart's past.

"I told him that it's funny how Rim Bolden always seems to find some excuse to go up to the big house when Mrs. Stallart's to home and Stallart ain't."

"And what did Stallart say to that?"

"He looked a little worried. But he just said that Bolden likely had things to talk over with Mrs. Stallart." Jellick suddenly laughed. "You should've seen his face when I said, 'Seems to me I remember the first Mrs. Stallart gettin' visited like that back in Kansas.'"

"That should give him something to think about," Ward said, and rubbed his narrow brown hands together.

"Stallart sorta dug a finger into his throat when I mentioned Kansas," Jellick chuckled. "Like he wanted to make sure it was his collar chokin' him and not a noose."

"Well, he knows you're working with me now." Ward's pale gaze hardened. "And he sure as hell can guess why I moved in next door to him."

"Don't forget," Jellick said, "that it was me who told you about Stallart. It was me that got you up here."

"I won't forget."

"How soon do you figure to start in on him?" Jellick wanted to know. "Ain't no use beatin' around the bush no more. He knows now for sure that we're out to get him."

"We'll start soon," Ward told him. "I have some boys coming out from town. We'll start with a couple hundred head and see how much he squeals."

"And I hope Rim Bolden's the one that comes lookin' for them cows."

Ward thoughtfully sipped his drink for a moment. "Damned funny," he said, "but in every plan there seems to be one sour note."

"You mean Rim Bolden?"

Ward nodded. "Everything was perfect when we first planned this last year. We could drain Stallart dry and he's too frightened of his neck to do anything about it. Then before I can get this thing rolling on greased axles he takes in Bolden as a partner."

"You'll get gray in the head worrying over little things," Jellick said. His right hand shot out and captured a lazy bottle-fly that was on the rim of his tin cup that held the whisky. He put the frantically buzzing insect against the table and flattened it with his thumb. "That's the way it'll be with Rim Bolden."

"Just remember this," Ward said evenly. "Don't try some hero play and beat him up in front of the town. He went through the war on the side that didn't know when to quit. Just make sure of him. With a gun."

"A grudge fist fight is better. It'll give me more pleasure. And Sheriff Dort won't be wonderin' about it."

"We're not in this for your pleasure or mine. We're in it for profit. Let's neither of us forget it."

"And if I gun him maybe the sheriff will say it was on account of me stealin' Anchor cows and Bolden comin' after me—"

"You liked the idea a minute ago. You said you hoped it was Bolden who came after you."

"Don't hurt none for a man to think about his neck," Jellick said. "Maybe the sheriff's on our side of the fence. Then maybe he ain't.

"You leave that to me."

Jellick was silent a moment, then said, "The way you got things fixed now we won't have to work over the brands at all like we figured at first."

"This way is even better," Ward said. "Now that I can see how frightened Stallart is."

"You sure got him reined in short and tight."

"Try and wait till we take the cows," Ward said. "Then you fix Rim Bolden. Don't chance getting in close with him. Use a rifle. We'll say he tried to steal back those cows."

Jellick leaned back in his chair, put his feet on the table. Ward, frowning with disapproval at the manure caked soles of the boots, moved the whisky bottle aside.

"There's one other thing to remember, Meade," Ward said. "Let's forget any more talk about Mrs. Stallart and Rim Bolden."

"I ain't workin' there no more, so how could I talk even if I want to? What good would it do?"

"I know that," Ward said with faint impatience. "I mean don't say anything about it in town. Let the matter drop. Stallart has the idea in his mind. He'll do the rest. And maybe you won't have to try for Bolden after all. Maybe Stallart will do it for you."

"Or maybe Stallart will be the one dead."

"I'm counting on that eventually, one way or another." Ward frowned. "I'm sorry it seemed necessary to involve a lady like Mrs. Stallart in some ugly talk, but—" His voice trailed away and he thought of a year before the war when he went south to New Orleans and his horse broke a leg on the Natchez Trace in the worst downpour he had ever seen. He had been given shelter in a fine plantation house. He knew it was in such a place that Marcy Stallart had been raised. It was the only sad part of the war for him; that he had fought against such people. The gray-clad horse soldiers or riflemen he could slaughter without conscience. But occasionally one encountered a gentleman. That was the tragic part of the war. If the gentlemen of both sides could only have joined in cards or drinking and left the actual fighting to the underlings—

Ward considered himself a gentleman. And he vowed that even though he had never planned to take as his wife a widow, he knew in the case of Marcy Stallart there was no choice. Since their first brief meeting on the street in LaVentana last month he knew he would have her. And it was too bad that she had to become involved in this at all. But he would make it up to her in many ways. And help her forget the nightmare of living with a man like Bert Stallart who was so obviously beneath her.

He had written his half-sister April, in Kansas, and told her he would like her to meet him. And when he drove his herd to Kansas she would return to New Mexico with him. April could make friends with the widow Stallart and this would ease the tension considerably—

"Wonder what Stallart's niece looks like when she ain't all puffed out like a hoss that's eaten green hay."

"Don't get involved with her whatever you do. We have enough obstacles as it is."

Jellick laughed. "You never just know how things is goin' to turn out."

"Let's keep our minds on cows. Not on women."

"You been sayin' Marcy Stallart's name in your sleep," Jellick said, his gaze narrowing. "Seems to me that's a damn far piece from thinkin' about the beef business."

Ward, flushing, poured himself another drink.

CHAPTER FIVE

For two days Bert Stallart did not take a drink and Rim began to feel a lessening of tensions around Anchor. Rim knew it stemmed from the birth of the boy that Stallart intended to raise as his own. At least, Rim thought, he could thank Ellamae for that much. Providing she was willing to give up the boy. But he didn't worry too much about that. He sensed that Stallart would have his own way. Since the night of Ellamae's arrival Rim had not seen Marcy Stallart. Neither had he seen Ellamae.

Stallart spent several hours a day just looking at the boy. He would tell Rim how he seemed to be growing already. How he had a smart look in his eye for a young'un. "By God, Rim," Stallart said this morning, "the boy favors my brother Paul—" And then, at mention of his brother, Stallart's eyes got that haunted look again, and he glanced hurriedly over his shoulder as if to see if an enemy lurked close by.

On several occasions Rim had started to ask about Paul Stallart, then decided against it. After all, it was none of his business. Not unless it in some way became a threat to Anchor.

But Rim did say on this night, three days since the birth of the boy, "Why don't you name him Paul, after your brother?"

They were in Rim's office-bedroom discussing the roundup that was due to start in a few weeks. Stallart got up from the cot where he had been sitting. His eyes were no longer bloodshot, and his breath did not reek of whisky.

"Reckon I'll name the boy Grant," Stallart said, and looked away. "After our president."

He went out, leaving Rim alone. Rim felt a return of the old tensions. He tried to work on the books, but couldn't make much sense out of the figures. He was thinking how, in the past weeks, his partnership with Stallart seemed to be getting mighty tenuous. It was nearly a year since Rim had come here to Anchor. He thought he knew Stallart, about as well as one partner could know another. But lately he felt that Stallart was a stranger. And Marcy, who used to laugh so much, now seemed despondent.

Rim was worried.

He was about to shuck his clothes and try to sleep when he heard a light knock on the door. Rim went over and opened it. Marcy burst in, looking distraught. "Bert—Bert—" Then she turned and looked at Rim. "One of the men said Bert was in here with you."

Rim saw her eyes swollen from weeping. "He just left."

She passed a hand over her eyes. "Oh, Rim—" She wore a cloak that was unbuttoned and moccasins. When she swayed, Rim sprang forward and caught her. "Oh, Rim, I tried," she whispered hoarsely. "I really tried—"

The door opened suddenly and Bert Stallart walked in, his face gray. Rim's gaze involuntarily flashed to his gun rig hanging from a wall hook.

"I was at the cookshack," Stallart said, his voice steel sharp. "I seen you come in here, Marcy—"

She whirled into the circle of her husband's arms. "Bert, we—we'll have a burial tomorrow—"

Stallart stiffened and some of the rage left his eyes. He held his wife at arm's length and peered down into her wet face. "So she died," he breathed.

"I'm sorry," Rim said.

"Reckon it's like my pa used to say," Stallart said gravely. "There ain't nothin' worse than a sinning woman. And she pays for it every time." He took a bandanna from his hip pocket and blew his nose. "I 'member her once when I went East years back. She was a pretty little yellow-haired thing. Never thought she'd one day have a bastard kid—"

"Bert, don't say that about the boy," Marcy cried softly.

Something in her voice stiffened Stallart's shoulders. "It is Ellamae, ain't it? It's her dead?"

"The boy," Marcy sobbed. "I tried to save him, Bert." She shook her dark head wearily. "I tried. I really tried."

Stallart stood for a moment with his head bowed. Or at least Rim thought this was what he was doing in a moment of reverence. Then he was aware that Stallart glared at him from under bushy brows.

"Marcy," Stallart said in a shaking voice, "I don't never want to find you in Rim's bedroom again."

"Bedroom?" Marcy said, looking up. "This is the office—Bert, I came here to find you. To tell you about the boy."

Stallart's mouth twisted and he looked at his wife. There was hurt and bewilderment in her eyes.

"You mind what I said," Stallart grunted. He gave her a shove toward the door. "Seems like I stand in the shadow of a black star. I had plans for that boy—" His voice broke.

"Be thankful your niece survived, at least," Rim reminded him.

This seemed to jar Stallart. "Marcy, get her out of my house. To-night!"

Marcy dashed a hand across her eyes as if to clear them of tears. "I thought you had a heart as big as this whole of New Mexico. It's one of the things I loved about you, Bert. Don't tell me you'd do this thing."

Stallart stared hard at her, then swung his gaze to Rim. "Remember this. We share some of the profits of this ranch. We don't share nothing else."

Rim felt a rush of heat to his face. He took a step toward Stallart, but saw the swift pleading in Marcy's eyes. He drew up, lowered the fist he had clenched.

"Come to bed, Bert," she said in a voice taut with strain. "It's been a trying day."

Before he went to sleep that night he disassembled his revolver and gave it a thorough cleaning. Then he loaded it and placed it on a chair beside his bed.

They had the burial in the morning. The skies were dark and dripped rain and above the Mogollon Rim lightning flashed like a writhing snake against the wet trees. Stallart, stone-faced, stood with bowed head. Marcy was dry-eyed. Rim Bolden could not remember much of the Scripture his mother had read to him, so he improvised.

He said, "Lord, this boy stayed only a short time in our world. He didn't have a chance to do right or wrong. Help him."

Two roustabouts filled in the grave. Rim put on his hat, turned toward the house. He saw Ellamae's face briefly at an upstairs window. He felt sorry for her, sorrier than he had ever felt for anyone in his life.

"What name shall I put on the headboard, Bert?" Rim asked.

"A bastard has no name," Stallart said bitterly and moved down the slant away from the Anchor burial ground. There were other graves beside that of the boy. There was the horsebreaker who had been crushed against the corral fence by a fractious horse last spring; the cowhand who had succumbed to the results of a brief exposure to a blanket woman who had come down from the hills; another Anchor hand had been gored by a pecky cow who charged him with eyes open while he was dismounted. Rim had a feeling on this bleak day that before his association with Anchor was terminated there would be more graves on the knoll behind the house.

Marcy came close to Rim, her dark gaze serious. "I want Bert to give her enough money so she can go somewhere and make a new life for herself. Will you do all you can to persuade him?"

"I'll try," he promised, but he knew Stallart would not listen to him. He walked down to the house with Marcy.

Bert Stallart came up suddenly behind them. "You two are almighty quiet," he said, his eyes strangely bright.

"That was a senseless thing to say," Marcy snapped. She went into the house.

Stallart and Rim eyed each other. The men, saddling up down at the corral, were watching them. And Rim knew what was going on in most of their minds. These were days when a man sometimes rode fifty miles to get a job and when he got there found there had been maybe ten ahead of him. Two partners having trouble could mean disaster. It could mean the end of a ranch such as Anchor, and that in turn would mean the end of their jobs.

"We're not doing each other any good by this, Bert," Rim said, holding himself in for Marcy's sake.

Stallart said, "What about you and my wife?"

"Marcy is a fine woman. I respect her. Somebody is trying to make some ugly talk. I have a hunch it was Meade Jellick."

At mention of the horsebreaker's name Stallart looked away toward the hills. "You shouldn't have fired him. Not without talking it over with me first."

"You're afraid of him, Bert. Why?"

Stallart wheeled to face Rim again, his hands clenched. "I ain't scared of no man on this earth. You better believe that."

"Bert, when we sell some beef we'd better dissolve our partnership."

"Yeah, reckon," Stallart said and stomped on down to the corral.

For the rest of the week there was feverish activity at Anchor; so many things to do before roundup. The chuckwagon was set up on blocks, the wheels pulled, the axles greased. A rent in the canvas top was mended. Because there were still horses to break for roundup, Rim took over the task vacated by Jellick. Rim rode down to the horse camp with Willie Temple. He put Marcy's brother in charge. When Willie began to strut and cuss out the men in his new importance, Rim warned him.

"Don't get too big for your hat, Willie, or we'll have to shrink your head a little."

Rim took the pounding in the breaking corral. He risked having his legs smashed against the wall of the circular pen. Twice he stepped down just in time to prevent a back-falling mount from crashing down on him. Since the funeral he saw very little of Bert Stallart. When he ate with the men in the cookshack the talk was spare. There was a minimum of joshing.

Ed Rule got him aside one morning when the hands had taken their assignments for the day's work and gone out. "Saw Tut Tyler in town yesterday when I went in for supplies," the old cook said. "He ain't happy working for Ward. He wants to come back."

"He made his choice," Rim said, and helped himself to his third cup of coffee.

"Yeah, but sometimes a man ain't as bad as he seems. Tyler took a five dollar gold piece from Eric Ward to come out and tell Jellick about you and Ward tangling. And about Stallart's niece being all swole up with the kid. He didn't figure it was being disloyal to Anchor."

"I could never trust him again, Ed."

"All the boys sort of miss Tyler around here. He always had something funny to say of a morning. Kind of got the day started right, if you know what I mean."

Rim finished his coffee. With an expert aim he tossed the cup into the big pan beyond the table. "You might as well know the truth, Ed. When Stallart gets enough cash to buy out my interest, I'm through here."

Ed Rule fingered the grease-spattered apron tucked into his belt. "I can tell you this, Rim. Tough as jobs are to come by, there's a lot of us would follow you. Stallart ain't an easy man to work for these days."

"Bert's all right."

"Some of us don't like the way he's treated his niece. Sure, the girl done wrong. But it's a failing of us humans. We all done wrong in our lives, one way or another."

Rim got up, conscious of the weight of a gun dragging his belt. Usually around the home ranch he wore no weapon, feeling it to be an affectation. But since the episode with Jellick and the growing hostility between himself and Bert Stallart, he had altered his thinking.

"Ed, we're going to have trouble at roundup. I feel it. Ward is going to try and widen the chasm between Stallart and me. This business of Mrs. Stallart and—" Rim broke off, feeling disgust that Stallart would believe such vicious gossip.

"I've knowed Stallart a lot longer than you have, Rim," Ed Rule said quietly, after looking around to make sure that no one was within earshot. The men were riding out, some of them instructed by Rim to make a wide circle and see if they could note any unusual activity on the part of their nearest neighbor, Eric Ward.

"Stallart was married before," Ed Rule said.

Rim looked around at the old cook. "I didn't know that."

"Some girl in Kansas. He never talked much about it. But a time or two he got kind of heavy with whisky and he unburdened himself, so to speak. He caught this wife of his with somebody else and there was a killing."

"Who was the man?"

"Stallart never told me. When he sobered up he made me swear I'd never say nothing about it. But I figure you ought to know, Rim. Maybe you can understand now why Stallart is so all-fired easy to sway with talk about you and Marcy."

"Everything in Stallart's life seems to point back to Kansas. He knew Jellick there."

"I told you what I know about that, Rim." Ed Rule shook his gray head. "Stallart had bad luck with one marriage. A thing like that primes a man to look for the worst in a woman, if somebody is nudging him just right."

"A man has tough luck with a horse," Rim said. "It doesn't mean he's going to be afoot for the rest of his life just because one horse went bad on him."

"There's hell shapin' up, Rim. I got a bad feeling about it."

"So have I."

CHAPTER SIX

Rim took three men and rode up on ridges to see if he could see any of T's riders. But they saw nothing. In this country it was customary for one rancher to notify another concerning roundup camps to be established. Only Sabers, to the west of Anchor had sent over a rep to say that if it was all right with Stallart and Rim Bolden, first camp would be on the West Fork of the Gila.

Rim had seen no objection to that and asked Stallart for his opinion. Stallart grunted something and stalked away. Rim told the Sabers rep that he would be there with his crew at the designated time.

Today Rim was on the way back to Anchor headquarters after his fruitless scouting expedition when one of the men, Rupe Simpson, swung his horse over to Rim's dun. Simpson had been chewing a ropy cigar for the past hour.

"I'm plumb outa fire, Rim," he said, his long sunburned face smiling. "Could you give me the loan of a match?"

Rim was staring down through a dense thicket of jack-pines. His dun's ears were twitching and he felt a sudden tenseness in the air. The other two men were slightly ahead and to Rim's right. They rode with stirrups touching, and their conversation concerned the talent Daisy would import from Mesilla and Paso for the week or so following roundup when everyone sort of relaxed.

Simpson leaned close to take the match Rim held out for him. Rim was watching the trees ahead. Simpson said, "Thanks," and the ears of Rim's dun twitched again.

Simpson struck the match on the worn underside of his saddlehorn and at that moment, Rim said, "Watch it, boys."

He didn't know why he voiced the warning, save that his nerves were keyed up. If you spooked every time your horse showed a twitching at the ears you could dismounted half the time with a rifle in your hands. Because it could be a bob cat in the trees, or a bear, or just a saddle bum that could cause a horse to be jumpy.

When Rim spoke Simpson looked up to see why he had voiced the warning. The match was flaming and the heat scorched the tips of his fingers. Swearing, he involuntarily dropped the match. It struck the right foreleg of Rim's dun. The horse leaped, all four hoofs off the ground. Its tail swung around, sideswiping Simpson's bay. Simpson, leaning far over in the saddle, was forced to grab the horn to keep from being spilled.

Rim was fighting down his dun, looking back at Simpson. He saw the bridge of Simpson's nose explode in that moment. Saw a flying splinter of white bone no larger than the end of a man's little finger. And then as Simpson was falling, there came the crash of a heavy rifle from some point deep in the jackpines ahead. Simpson's bay lunged frantically and its rider went sideways out of the saddle, the right foot caught solidly in the stirrup. As Rim drew his rifle, the bay cut crazily across his dun's nose, sending the horse into another fit of bucking.

"Take cover!" Rim was yelling, but the other two men didn't have to be told. They broke their horses apart, dragging up rifles from saddle boots.

They began firing indiscriminately into the jackpines. With his dun at last under control, Rim sat in his saddle, scanning the trees.

He swallowed and his throat was suddenly sand-dry. "Save your shells!" he cautioned the men. No more shots came from the trees. He signaled the two men and they drove in spurs and quickly reached the shelter of some large boulders at the base of a brushy hill.

The bay horse was still running and as it made a wide swing, the foot of its rider became dislodged. Simpson rolled loosely.

"Get the horse," Rim ordered. Then, rifle in hand, he rode slowly into the trees. The hoofbeats of a running horse came to him faintly. At last he found where the ambusher had stood. The prints of the two boots were large. He saw where the man had swung into the saddle and ridden quickly to the north. He followed the tracks for a quarter of a mile; tracks made by a big horse, carrying a big man. The tracks led toward broken country where it would be hard to trail. One ambush a day was enough, and he had no intention of running into a second.

When he rode back he was drenched with sweat. He peered down at Simpson who looked now like a dusty torn sack of clothing. Rim never got used to a sight like this. A boyhood in Texas where death was as common as Sunday, four years of war had never conditioned him. There was no way at all to identify the man on the ground if they hadn't known who he was. The face was gone, scraped on hard ground and rock.

The man bending over Simpson's body was white about the mouth. He was a kid, Charlie Daws, the youngest hand at Anchor, next to Willie Temple, Marcy's brother. "He's dead," the kid said, awed.

"Dead before he hit the ground," Rim said. He put a hand to his face, feeling his strong bony nose against the palm of his hand. There but for the grace of God—

"Who done it?" Charlie Daws asked in a shaking voice.

"A big man on a big horse," Rim said and hoped the younger man didn't notice the tremor in his voice. It was the same as it had been in the war. You led your men, and even though you wanted to turn to the nearest bush and empty your guts because of the things you'd seen, you had to act tough. You had to act as if one man dead or a hundred made no difference. You were in a fight and if the men felt you as their leader were frightened, what would it do to their morale?

"You mean Jellick done this?" the second man said. He was Tom Niles, a swarthy man with a scar that made a white cross on his right cheek.

"Jellick had nothin' against Simpson," Charlie Daws said. "He only—"

"It's only a guess about Jellick," Rim said, putting ice in his voice. "But a good one. He wasn't shooting at Simpson. He was shooting at me." Rim looked toward the trees. Green branches stirred quietly in the breeze that had come up. It was hard to realize that deep in that greenery had lurked a rifleman with death in his sights.

Charlie Daws looked angry. "You don't seem to give much of a damn whether Simpson is dead or not."

"Listen, kid," Rim said. "It's over and done. Thing to do now is to get back to headquarters."

They came in at sundown with the body of Simpson slung over the back of the bay he had ridden out that morning. By lantern light they had a second funeral.

Stallart said, when the brief ceremony was over, "How the hell do you know it was Jellick?" And when Rim told his partner about the tracks, Stallart said, "That don't mean nothing. Maybe some fella was packing a grudge for Simpson. Card game, or a woman or anything—"

"You don't want me going after Jellick, is that it?"

"I never said that," Stallart muttered. "But good God, Rim, you got to have proof."

"If I killed Jellick," Rim said quietly, "then you'd no longer have him on your back."

Stallart had started for the house where lamplight spilled from the windows and touched the hoof-packed yard. He swung back. "What'd you mean by that?" he demanded hoarsely.

"Jellick wouldn't be around to hold it over you," Rim said. "Whatever it was that you did back in Kansas."

Stallart made a low, strangling sound in his throat. And Rim was on his guard, half-expecting the man to lash out with a heavy fist. But the steam seemed to suddenly go out of Stallart. He dropped his hands. "Stay away from Jellick. It's my doings and I'll handle it in my own way."

"Your way may not be the right one. Simpson was our man. He's dead. You going to let them get away with that?"

"We got a sheriff, haven't we?" Stallart snapped.

"Yes, we have. I'll go into town tomorrow and have a talk with him."

"If you're going to town," Stallart said angrily, "you can drive in that woman. She's stayed here too long as it is."

Since the unfortunate night when Ellamae had appeared at the ranch Stallart always referred to her as *that woman.*

In the morning Rim had the wagon driven up to the cookshack by one of the hands. Then with belted gun, and rifle and shotgun lashed in boots tied to the seat braces, Rim called for Ellamae. She came out of the house, wearing the cloak and the bonnet. The cloak fit her loosely now. Without a word she climbed into the wagon. Marcy came out, her dark eyes worried.

"Good-by, Ellamae," she said. "Write to me."

"I'll pay you back, Marcy," Ellamae said, without looking at her. "Every cent."

Marcy looked quickly around the yard, her eyes concerned. "Please. I told you never to let on. I don't want—"

"You don't want your fine husband to know you gave me a few dollars," Ellamae said, her lips curling. "Don't worry."

"Good luck, Ellamae."

"One thing he can't take from me," the girl said bitterly. "My name. It's Stallart, the same as his. I'm going to make him proud of the name. Real proud."

She blew her nose as Rim drove her out. "Uncle Bert could've taken me when I was a kid. When my father died. But he didn't. He left me in Joplin with that woman he called Aunt Rosie. I never had a chance to be anything decent, Rim."

"Most of us never had much of a chance. But most of us make out one way or another."

"There's never been a woman who's suffered like me."

"I remember a woman in Atlanta. Raped by a bunch of drunken soldiers. She said, 'Rim, when the war is over I'll make a new life.' And she did."

"I don't believe you." She clenched her small hands. He could see the faint down on her cheeks. "When I felt my baby coming I wanted to be something good. I—I thought maybe even you'd marry me. Although I suppose that was the craziest thing a woman could ever think."

"I don't love you, Ellamae. If I did it might not make any difference—about the baby. I don't know. A man never knows those things until he's faced with it."

They went the rest of the way in silence. In LaVentana he cramped the wagon against a hitchrail and tied the team. "I'll buy you a stage ticket if you'll tell me where you're going."

Ellamae gave him a frozen smile. "I don't intend to go anywhere. I'll stay here. Right in LaVentana."

Without a backward glance she swept into the lobby of the hotel, her skirts raising a small cloud of dust.

Rim shrugged. Well, it was none of his affair. As he had all along he felt sorry for her. But she wasn't going to gain anything if she tried to get back at her Uncle Bert. Better that she take the money Marcy had given her and try to make a fresh start. He knew the folly of vengeance. He'd tried to live with it in Texas after the war, but he grew tired of those men whose lives were dedicated to the reliving of the war, saying if this hadn't happened, or that happened, or the damned British, or Lee not being where he should have been or Pickett making his senseless infantry charge when any fool knew that if you put a horse under a man he was twice as formidable. On and on—Wait till next year, boys. There'll be another rebellion, wait and see. This one'll be a success—

Rim walked down to the sheriff's office. He found Sheriff Jared Dort shaping a piece of clay into an Indian head. It was a fairly good job, Rim had to admit. Dort looked around, his hands dripping from the tin basin he had been dipping them in.

"Surprised to see you in town, Bolden," Dort grunted. "Ain't you boys started roundup yet?"

Rim leaned against a table the sheriff used as his desk. "I've got something important to talk about."

"Well, talk ahead," Dort grumbled. He kept fussing with the nose of the clay head he was working on.

"I watched a man's nose splintered under a rifle shell yesterday," Rim said.

CHAPTER SEVEN

Jared Dort's back stiffened. "Who got shot?"

Rim swallowed his irritation. Dort didn't afford him a spare glance even. Since coming here last year Rim had sensed the sheriff's unfriendliness, but had been unable to find a basis for it.

Rim told about the shooting of Simpson. He described the sign he had found where the ambusher had fired his shot and then ridden off. Still Dort said nothing. He knew Dort had fought for the South, so this couldn't be the reason for his evident dislike.

"I'll stake my life that it was Meade Jellick," Rim said. "Trying for me. But he got Simpson by mistake."

"You got proof?" Dort dipped his hands in the tin basin and then began pressing his fingers into the soft clay.

"I just told you my proof," Rim said, trying to hold himself in.

"You call a few tracks proof?"

"It's good enough for me."

"Ain't good enough for me," the sheriff retorted. "So don't take up my time."

"Yes, I can see you're *busy.*" Rim waved impatiently at the clay head. "But unless I'm mistaken we pay you for keeping the peace. Not for fooling with clay—"

Sheriff Dort looked around. He had a square face. His eyes under a brushy slope of brows were set deep in his skull. His hair as well as his mustache needed trimming. They said he had failed as a miner and rancher before somehow managing to get himself elected sheriff.

"You come in town the other day and you mess up one of our leading citizens," Dort said. "Eric Ward, I'm talkin' about. Now you come to me with some story about Meade Jellick killing one of your men."

"I can see I'm wasting my time."

"No, you're wasting *my* time!" Sheriff Dort snapped. "Hold on there, Bolden!"

Rim had started for the door. Now he looked around, waiting. Dort came up slowly, wiping his clay-smeared fingers on a dirty towel.

"You talk about proof," Dort said. "You goddam Texans don't know what proof means."

"So that's why you hate my guts. Because I'm from Texas."

"Lemme tell you about proof," Dort said. "When the war was two years done my brother—my kid brother—got away from some damn blue bellies that had him took prisoner. He was in his underwear and he stole a suit from a ranch house. He was trying to get back to his own side. But some of you goddam Texans full of Chisos Whisky, got him. They said he was a spy because he didn't have his uniform. They said they didn't need no proof. And they hung my kid brother. I been saving myself a hate for any Texan I seen from that day on. You see how I feel, Bolden?"

"I'm sorry about your brother. A lot of things happened in the war—"

"I wear this badge and I do what the job calls for. If you come in here with a witness that seen one man kill another I'll go after the killer. Don't come in here and tell me that just because you seen sign of a big hoss and a big man you got proof. Your goddam Texas proof don't mean a damn to me."

"There's going to be trouble hereabout, Dort," Rim said. "I just thought I'd let you know about it."

"You cut too wide a circle," the sheriff warned, shaking a moist forefinger, "and I'll get me the same kind of a Texas rope that killed my brother."

"I'm a property owner here, Dort. I help pay your salary. I'm not going to be pushed by anybody, understand?"

"You speaking for Bert Stallart or just yourself?"

"Both of us."

"Well, I wonder about that." Dort picked at a piece of clay stuck to his jaw. "A lot of folks never could figure why Bert Stallart would take you in as a partner."

"That's Stallart's business—and mine!"

Rim walked out. Even though the spring sun was warm he felt as if he'd been drenched with ice water. He didn't even go to the saloon for a drink. He bought a bottle at the store, then drove for Anchor. Outside town he uncorked the bottle and took a long pull. He felt that this had been a very bad day. It had been a very bad two weeks, when you stopped to think about it. Everything seemed to go to hell from the moment Ellamae Stallart, heavy with child, stepped out of the stage coach in LaVentana.

Five miles along the road he saw a horseman angling for the road. The rider, on a gray, cut down from some aspens growing close to the hills. Without taking his eyes from the rider Rim reached down and with one hand freed his rifle from the boot lashed to the seat brace. Then he recognized the rider. It was Tut Tyler.

Rim drew in the team as Tyler came up. Tyler was sweating more than he should have been. "Howdy," Tyler said, and his grin was forced.

Rim's gaze ran over the gray horse, seeing Ward's T brand on the flank.

"Didn't take you long to sign on," Rim observed. "Sign on regular, I mean."

Tyler flushed. "I don't like the way things is shaping up, Rim. I—Simpson was a friend of mine."

Rim hesitated. "Then you know who shot him?"

Tyler fiddled with his reins. "I'd like to be back working with Anchor."

"You didn't answer me," Rim pressed. "You know who shot Simpson?"

"I want to be on your side of the fence. That's all I can say."

"It was Meade Jellick," Rim said. "He was trying for me and he got Simpson by mistake."

"Yeah—yeah, reckon that's true."

"I want Jellick. I'd like to see Jellick hang, if there's a rope in this country big enough to do the job." Rim leaned forward. "Will you go back to town with me and tell Sheriff Dort that it was Jellick?"

"A man might as well put the muzzles of that shotgun you got slung to the seat there, Rim, in his mouth and work the trigger with his big toe. You're dead any way you look at it."

"It takes more guts to face up to the truth, than it does to blow your own head off."

"I'm sick of Ward. You goin' to take me back, Rim?"

"How would I know you're to be trusted?"

"You got my word."

"I'll think about it, Tyler," Rim said. He put the rifle back in the boot under the seat. "When is Ward going to start roundup?"

"He don't figure to hold a roundup, Rim."

This caused Rim to lift his brows. The rancher in country like this who didn't hold roundup twice a year, didn't stay in business very long. But he knew Ward was too smart for that.

"I'll ask you again about Jellick," Rim said. "Tell your story to the sheriff. You'll have Anchor behind you."

Tyler shook his head. "I'll come back to work and I'll work like hell to make up—Rim, I never meant nothing when I told Jellick about you fighting with Ward in town. And about that niece of Stallart's all swole up—"

"Did Jellick admit that he killed Simpson? I know there was nobody else with him because of the sign. Just one rider. But—"

"Jellick done some cussing that night. He had you dead center, he said, then something spooked your hoss and he missed. He lit outa there because he said you was three to one and he didn't like fighting them odds."

"Simpson asked me for a match. He dropped it, burning, and it hit my horse. It was just that little thing that meant I'm alive and Simpson is dead. If he was your friend you should want to see Jellick hang for killing him."

"Rim, I seen Jellick one time at Mesilla. He was drunk and mean and he got in a fight with a big teamster. He took this teamster across his knee and busted his back like a stick. It'd be bad enough if he'd just take a gun. But I know him. He'd kill me and take a long time doing it."

"You don't seem to think the law or Anchor offers much protection to a man like you."

Tyler rubbed his jaw. "I don't know about Anchor, but with Sheriff Dort—Well, he's goin' to lean mighty heavy on anybody that tries to cut the ground out from under Ward's outfit."

Rim felt he was touching on something. "Is there some connection between Ward and the sheriff?"

Tyler looked surprised. "Dort's brother buys the beef for Fort Slaughter up north of here. That's how come Ward got the beef contract—I figured you knew that, Rim."

"No. First time I heard about it." The knowledge that the sheriff had used his influence to get Eric Ward a beef contract was unsettling. "It's unethical for a man holding public office to use his influence—" Rim broke off, knowing he wasted his breath. Not many men cared for a sheriffing job in country like this. The townspeople and the other ranchers wouldn't take kindly to having Dort put under a cloud. Particularly not at the start of roundup. This was a time for tension; and no time for a new sheriff to take over.

"Have you ever heard Jellick or Ward, for that matter, mention any business they might have had with Bert Stallart back in Kansas?" Rim asked.

"Never heard nothing, Rim." Tyler licked his lips. He was still sweating too much. "Guess you're goin' to turn me down. About the job, I mean."

Rim made up his mind. "I just can't take a chance. Not now. I've got to count on my men."

Color flooded into Tyler's face again. Without a word he turned his horse and sent it at a dead run for the aspens growing at the foot of the hills.

Rim pushed his team more than was his custom, because even armed with a rifle for long work and a shotgun for up-close fighting he was vulnerable. In case Tyler rode to a nearby T camp and told the men there he had just seen Rim Bolden.

CHAPTER EIGHT

For one of the few times since his life started at Anchor, Willie Temple felt important. Rim had put him in charge of the remuda, which was to be moved from the horse camp to the roundup headquarters on the Gila. There were nearly a hundred head of horses that he and four Anchor riders were to push north and west to roundup camp. It was the day after Rim returned from town. Willie knew there had been a scene at the house last night, Stallart yelling that Ellamae had no right to stay in LaVentana. She should get out where her disgrace could not blacken the Stallart name. Willie heard his sister trying to quiet her husband, but Stallart bellowed like a bull with a horn broken off short.

And Willie noticed that Rim seemed mighty sour these days. Rim usually had a word for you. He would fan your tail with work during the day but at night he'd have a drink and some cards with the boys in the bunkhouse. But not now. The word had gotten around that once they sold off some beef Rim was going to take enough to pay for his partnership and clear out. Willie hated for this to happen. Rim being at Anchor was the only thing that made it tolerable.

That morning Willie made a great show of looking over the remuda. The horses were all broken, most of them by Meade Jellick. The rest of the string had the rough corners knocked off by Rim Bolden.

One of the men with Willie that morning was Sam Englander. Although Rim had given orders that there was to be no drinking from the start of roundup to the finish, Willie knew that Englander had a bottle hidden out behind the horse camp. Englander made frequent trips down to the brush to "run a little water on the ground," he said.

Willie, in his Natchez drawl, said, "You all better swap bladders with the next cow we butcher. Yours is in need of repair." He laughed, thinking this was a huge joke.

Englander's round red face was lacking in humor. But Willie forgot about the hand as he made ready to drive the horses through the pass and to the roundup camp.

Englander made his final trip into the brush and Willie was surprised when he came hurrying back. He drew in his bay horse, showering pine needles. He gestured wildly behind him.

"Know what I just seen, Willie?" he cried.

"A purple snake wearing a red hat," Willie said.

"Goddam you, Willie—" Englander showed his anger.

"You been drinking enough to see most anything."

"I just seen about two hundred head of Anchor cows."

"This is Anchor ranch," Willie said, feeling a slight uneasiness. "Why wouldn't there be Anchor cows?"

"Meade Jellick and six boys was pushin' 'em toward Eric Ward's place over the hill." Englander gestured toward the south.

"Jellick isn't fool enough to do that," Willie said, and there was a thread of doubt in his voice.

"Go see for yourself," Englander said. "I watched 'em from the ridge yonder."

And now Willie and the other three men, who had come up from the corrals at the sound of Englander's excited voice, looked in the direction the cowhand had pointed. There was a big cloud of dust looming up as the bunch of cattle obviously were driven out of the trees and onto the flats where the dust was thick.

As Willie watched the dust cloud grow, he was weighted with indecision. He was about to tell one of the men to ride over to the Gila Camp where Rim would be this morning. But at that moment he heard a slow-moving horse and saw Bert Stallart coming up from the direction of the dust cloud.

"You saw them, Bert?" Willie asked his brother-in-law.

"Saw what?" Stallart said and rose up in his stirrups and peered over the corral fence at the horses bunched there. "You better be getting these on the trail. Rim'll be needing 'em tomorrow."

Willie felt a taut anger. The four men at the camp exchanged quick glances, then shook their heads as if unable to understand Stallart's attitude.

Willie walked over to where Stallart sat his horse. "Englander says there's two hundred head of our cows being driven off by Meade Jellick."

Stallart's face this morning was strangely lacking in color. He swallowed and gave Willie an impatient glance. "You mind your own goddam business, Willie."

"You mean you're letting Jellick—"

A bright steel anger flashed across Stallart's eyes. "I said mind your own business!"

Willie stood stiffly, all the dislike he held for this man his sister had married churning through him. In that moment he felt his frustrations keenly. He knew Marcy had married to give him a home, as much as herself. And he secretly knew that if it hadn't been for Marcy taking Bert

Stallart as her husband he, Willie, would still be forking hay at the livery in LaVentana.

"Willie," Stallart said coldly, "Rim gave you a job to do. Get at it!"

Stallart started to swing his horse away from the corral fence and spur it toward Anchor headquarters three miles away. But Willie caught the horse by the bridle, bringing it up short. Stallart's gun leaped into his hand. He laid the long barrel against Willie's forehead, breaking the skin. There was a bright gushing redness across Willie's face as he dropped heavily. Half-conscious he lay there, unable to move, seeing the hoofs of Stallart's prancing horse come dangerously close to his skull.

"Tell him," he heard Stallart say to the men, "that if he ever lays hand on me or my horse again, I'll kill him!"

This reached Willie through the roaring pain in his head. He rolled over. Englander helped him to sit up and was pressing a bandanna to his forehead. Stallart was gone.

"What the hell's ailing him?" Willie said shakily. "He gone crazy?"

"It's a wonder," one of the men said, "your brains ain't layin' on the ground beside the yellow pile his hoss just laid."

Englander got some of the blood wiped off Willie's forehead. "The boss ain't been right in the head since that gal showed up lookin' big around as a barrel."

Willie managed to get to his feet. "You got any of that whisky left, Englander?"

Englander wadded up the bloody bandanna and walked down to the creek that flowed beyond the largest of the two corrals. Over his shoulder, he said, "I finished it, Willie. Wish I had some to give you, but—"

Willie closed his eyes. His head felt as if an ax bit had split his skull. The ground was spinning and he thought he would fall down again. As his head gradually cleared he felt his dislike for Bert Stallart turn into a blinding hatred.

Here he was, segundo on Anchor. A man of importance, not some damned thirty dollar a month cowhand to be pistol-whipped. He treats me, Willie thought, like a horse he can't break. Whatever it is he can't dominate he wants to crush. Like my sister Marcy. Poor Marcy. If only Rim Bolden had come here to this country a year sooner—

Englander had washed out the bandanna and now came up to wipe the rest of the blood from the gash on Willie's forehead.

"This would be one hell of a lot better place to work," Willie said to Englander, "if Rim owned it instead of Bert Stallart."

"I s'pose," Englander said cautiously, as if not wanting to commit himself. "He sure give you a nasty cut on the forehead."

"If something happened to Bert Stallart," Willie said, grinding his teeth at the pain in his head, "Marcy and Rim would get married quick."

Englander said nothing. The other three men were saddling fresh horses down by the shack that was used for shelter at the camp.

"Stallart is playing some sort of a dirty game with Meade Jellick and Ward," Willie said, "And this business today with the two hundred head of cows proves it."

"Wa'al, maybe Stallart sold them cows—"

"He wouldn't sell Ward his second hand bath water for ten dollars a gallon." Willie took the wet bandanna from Englander and held it against the cut on his forehead. It helped ease the pain. "How many men did you say Jellick had with him?"

"Six, near as I could tell." Englander gave him a long look. "What you figurin' Willie?"

"I figure to get those cows back. They belong to Rim as much as they do to Bert Stallart."

Englander looked worried. He glanced down to the corral where the others were tightening cinches, as if he wished they were nearer to help him out. "I wouldn't go messin' with it, Willie, if I was you."

"Won't hurt to *ask* Mr. Jellick, just what the hell is going on."

"Maybe your memory done dried up after Stallart hit you, Willie. But I remember Rim and some of the boys ridin' in the other night with Simpson's body. Rim says Jellick killed him. I figure to stay alive a while longer."

"Look, Englander," Willie said sharply. "I'm segundo of this outfit. I take my orders from Rim. Not from Bert Stallart. Rim is foreman—"

"And Rim told you to get these hosses over to the Gila camp. Let's get at it—"

Englander started away, but Willie's voice arrested him. "If somebody's running off Anchor cows, it's our business to find out about it. That takes precedence over Rim's orders."

Englander looked puzzled, and Willie supposed he was trying to puzzle out what precedence meant. The other three hands came riding up. Willie told them what he planned to do. They didn't say anything, but looked at Englander as if expecting him to offer any objections.

But Willie spoke before Englander could say anything. "You all have good jobs here. I don't like Bert Stallart worth a damn and neither does any other man on the place if he'll speak the truth. There's a fight shaping up between Rim and Stallart. I'm choosing my side right now. It's Rim's. I'm segundo," Willie reminded again, looking at each man in turn, "and I have the right to give orders the same as Rim. But any man who doesn't want to follow my orders can get his time."

"Rim'll have something to say about that," Englander said stoutly.

"He'll back me up. He's not going to take kindly the rustling of two hundred head of beef that he has an interest in."

"So we find out Jellick's drivin' off Anchor beef. What can we do about it?" Englander said.

"We take them away from Jellick, that's what"

"But they're six—"

"Against our five." Willie gave as much a shake of the head as pain would allow. "I'm ashamed of you boys."

"I dunno," Englander said uneasily.

"I think it's going to be Stallart selling out his interest to Rim," Willie pressed on. "Instead of the other way around."

"And your sister will go with Stallart. I'll bet a wagonload of Carolina whisky against a bootful of side meat that's how it'll be, Willie. I know women—"

"She's my sister, goddam it, Englander. I should know her better than you do. Stallart isn't her kind of man at all. Rim is."

There was a sound over beyond the shack and the men turned in that direction. There was a sudden taut silence as they saw Bert Stallart standing there. He gripped a rifle.

"You whining, no-good son-of-a-bitch," Stallart said. "Get off my property, Willie! Get off or your guts will be bleeding on good Anchor ground."

Willie reacted strongly to the sudden appearance of his brother-in-law. Since the blow to the head his face had been without much color. But now it was completely pale. "You're cheating Rim," he accused, and hoped his voice was not shaking. "You are a thief!"

"I figured you'd talk when you come to," Stallart said, and started forward, his big feet making whispers of sound on the carpet of pine needles. The horses in the corral seemed to smell the tension for they began to mill. And the mounts of the three men sitting their saddles to one side of Willie and Englander began to fidget.

"Do you walk off this place, or do I drag you at the end of a rope?" Stallart cried.

Willie stood his ground as Stallart advanced out of the shadows thrown up by the shack. He saw Stallart work the loading lever of his rifle. Saw Stallart suddenly step from the shadows into bright sunlight that swept the yard. Stallart was facing into the morning sun and he involuntarily lifted a forearm to shade his eyes. And in that moment Willie made a desperate grab for his revolver. It surprised him even more than it did Stallart. One moment Stallart was standing tall, shaggy like the grizzly so many people had likened him to. Then Stallart was face down on the ground, head turned a little to one side. Dust stained his mustache and the brow and lashes of the eye turned toward Willie. The echoes of Willie's gunshot still slammed around the trees.

"He's dead, sure as hell," one of the men said, awed by what he had seen Willie accomplish.

"No he ain't," Englander said. He was the first to reach Stallart. "Looks like you got him chest-high, Willie, in a bad place."

"Carry him into the shack," Willie instructed. For the first time in his life he felt invincible. He looked down at his brother-in-law where the men had placed him on one of the bunks. Stallart's breathing was heavy. His eyes were closed. Willie opened Stallart's shirt and saw the ugly smear of blood. He wanted to vomit. He turned away and asked Englander to do the bandaging. Willie went outside and smoked a cigarillo, and each time he lowered the cigar his hand was trembling.

At last Englander came to the doorway. "Reckon he ain't so bad hit, Willie. 'Less blood poison sets in. You sliced a chunk out of his side."

"Then we can leave him for a spell," Willie said. "Let's go and get those cows."

"But—"

"You heard me," Willie said, a new ring of authority in his voice. Cigar clamped in his teeth he led the four men in the direction of the dust cloud. At Willie's order they spread out and moved ahead cautiously. And suddenly they came upon six men, dismounted, when they made a bend in the trail taken by the driven cattle. Each man held a rifle.

Willie's mouth opened in surprise and he dropped his cigar. And in that moment he realized that the gunshot, when he had downed Stallart, was what had alerted these men. But it was a little late for any thinking in this world for either Willie or the four Anchor men flanking him. Willie saw the jut of smoke from each rifle barrel, but he didn't hear the crash of the weapons an instant later. The ugly wound in his forehead suffered a deeper penetration than that caused by the revolver barrel swung by Bert Stallart earlier.

CHAPTER NINE

Rim was at the roundup camp, silently cursing Willie for not getting a move on with the remuda when Ed Rule, riding bareback on one of the mules usually hitched to the chuckwagon, tore into the clearing. The men, sensing trouble, streamed up. Across the river, which was little more than a creek here, the big Sabers camp was already set up. Smoke from cookfires curved like beckoning gray fingers against cliff walls.

It took the old cook a few moments to get his breath, after he slipped from the back of the sweat-streaked mule.

"I was comin' with the chuckwagon and I heard shooting over in the hills beyond the horse camp. I went over. Get hold of yourself, Rim."

"I've got a hold, Ed," Rim said grimly. "Is it Stallart?"

"Found him in the shack at the horse camp. Bad hit, I reckon. Anyhow he's unconscious. Then I went out to send Charlie Daws for help and I saw buzzards wheeling about a mile off. I rode over. Willie and the four boys who was going to drive the remuda over—all dead, Rim. Every one."

Rim felt the lash of grief. "Willie—dead—"

"Tracks of cows around, and riders, Rim. I—I don't want to figure what happened. I leave that up to you."

Rim looked around at the faces of his men and knew what they were thinking. This was a damn poor way for a man to die. Maybe earning twenty-five a month and his keep, with a horse furnished. And to go out and die to protect the cattle owned by his boss. And Rim knew that his premonition about more graves on the knoll behind the Anchor ranch house had been right. He cursed the black gloom that descended on him.

"Then Bert's the only one alive," Rim said, and marveled at the way he could control his voice in the face of crisis. But inside he was jelly. He saw the men watching him and he knew what they were thinking of him now: a cold-blooded bastard if there ever was one.

"I can't tell how bad Bert's been hit," Ed Rule said. "He's got a bandage but he's been bleeding bad. Charlie took him to the house. I come on here."

"Ed, you stay here and get your breath." Rim looked around. "Five men stay with him. The rest come with me."

They were a silent group of twenty riders moving swiftly along the wide cattle trail that led to Anchor. Here the sun was warm through the trees, and Rim could feel the warmth on his back. It was hard to realize that Willie would never feel anything again. Nor would any of the men with him. What had happened? was the thought that ripped constantly through his mind. What—in—hell—had—happened?

It took them hours to reach Anchor. As they pounded across the yard, raising a great clatter, he saw Marcy rush from the house, tears streaming from her eyes. Her hands were outstretched and Rim swung down and she came against him. "Oh, Rim—Rim—Willie dead. And Bert—"

"How is Bert? Is he conscious?"

"No. He hasn't spoken. Oh, Rim, what does it mean?"

Gently he pushed her away. The men were dismounted, staring. Nobody said a word.

Rim swallowed as he looked around. "I made a rule about whisky during roundup. Forget it. But not too much, understand? I have a feeling we'll do some riding tonight. Some of you go down and bring the bodies up here."

He went into the house.

"Oh, my God, Rim," Marcy said, her voice shaking. "This is awful. Willie missed going to war and I was so thankful his life was spared, and now—I lost three older brothers, Rim. Willie was the baby. I—" She began to laugh. She stepped away from him, head back, her eyes large flaming pools of black. Her laughter became a screech and he brought the flat of his hand against her face, knocking her aside. He sprang forward and caught her before she could fall.

"Marcy, Marcy," he said. He gripped her arms hard. He knew he was hurting her for he saw the writhing of her lips in pain. "We can't help Willie, but we can help Bert. Get hold of yourself."

"Yes, we must help Bert. How can you be so calm?"

"I learned calmness, Marcy. Four years of it. For four years I walked across a volcano on a greased fence rail. I had to learn calmness. It's something that comes with practice."

She pressed her eyeballs with the tips of her fingers as if to drain them of tears. Then she looked at him. "Maybe Bert has recovered consciousness. Maybe he can tell us—what happened."

They climbed the stairs and she no longer leaned on him. In that moment he thought she was the bravest woman he had ever known. Sunlight touched the landing and he thought back to the night of Ellamae's arrival. How Marcy, coming down these stairs to greet her husband's niece, had come to a halt, staring. Shocked by what she knew to be the truth about Ellamae and why she had come to "visit." But Marcy had quickly recovered even as she had recovered now, or partially so, from a greater shock. The death of her last brother.

Outside the door of the bedroom she shared with Bert Stallart she halted, put a finger against her lips. "We must be quiet."

She opened the door and they walked in. Bert Stallart had bunched his pillow behind him. There was a definite pallor on his heavy face. His hair seemed to be in a wilder tangle than usual. And the wildness was in his eyes. His gaze swung from his foreman, to his wife.

"You're better," Marcy cried, and started toward the bed. "You've regained consciousness—"

Then she came to a halt, her face losing color. Stallart had drawn a .45 from under his blanket. The cocking of the weapon was a lethal metallic sound in the quiet room.

"I was a mite under when Rule found me, I admit," Stallart said in that labored, painful way. "But I come to mighty quick. I been layin' up here. Thinkin'."

"You know about Willie?" Rim said.

"I know about Willie." Stallart bared his teeth, and the pain was a sickness in his eyes. But he managed to grin at them. There was a spot of redness along his left side under his shirt.

"We're going to have trouble, Bert," Rim said. "The ranch—"

"Damned right we're goin' to have trouble." Stallart gestured violently with the gun when Marcy tried to go to him. She shot Rim a bewildered glance. "Willie told me all about you two," Stallart went on.

"There's nothing to tell, Bert," Rim said, feeling a creeping iciness in the pit of his stomach. The cold eye of the gun Stallart held was centered on him now. The muzzle seemed big as a bear cave.

"One bullet to kill two sinful people," Stallart said.

Rim drew in a slow breath. "That wound has made you crazy, Bert."

"Willie told me how you two was fixin' to see me dead."

"No, Bert!" Marcy cried.

"I heard you laughin' downstairs a minute ago."

"Bert, I was hysterical," Marcy said, trying to still the trembling of her lips.

"Everybody knows you been sneaking up here to the house when my back's turned."

"No, Bert. Somebody's planted these ideas in your head."

"Willie told me right out. He said if I was dead you two would marry up."

"Willie's the one dead, Bert. Willie and Englander. And—" Rim named the other three men.

Stallart stared at him. "Get Willie up here. Let him deny he told me that."

"I've told you. Willie's dead."

"You're a liar." There was truly a touch of madness in the eyes now as his fingers tightened on the gun.

Rim suddenly sprang forward, launching himself at Marcy, and at the same time the bed. His hip struck Marcy, sent her flying. Stallart fired. The room rocked from the concussion of the exploding gun and Rim, as he dove for the bed, prayed to God the bullet wouldn't strike Marcy. He hit the floor heavily. Another shot screamed in an unholy voice of ricochet. Rim's shoulders were under the edge of the bed. He heaved up, tipping the bed. Stallart struck the wall with the crown of his head. He went limp.

Shakily Rim picked himself up, stared at his unconscious partner. He got Stallart's gun. He turned and saw Marcy crumpled on the floor, and for one terrible moment he thought one of the wildly fired bullets had struck its mark. Then she put out her hand and he helped her up.

She stood with head bowed, and he saw a tear make a bright star against the toe of her shoe.

"He didn't mean it, Marcy," Rim tried to say.

"He meant it."

Rim righted the bed as some of the men came pounding up the stairs, drawn by the shots. Rim went over and opened the door. "It's all right, boys. The boss is out of his head. I had to take a gun away from him."

Rim felt the men look at him, saw their eyes shift to the weeping Marcy. Then they looked at the great shaggy Bert Stallart lying twisted up in a gray blanket. A few of them exchanged glances and Rim knew what they were thinking. But he felt that to deny anything now would only make it worse.

"Help me with him, some of you," Rim ordered. And when the unconscious Stallart was back in the bed Rim got some strips of rawhide and tied each of Stallart's wrists to a rail of the bed. He told the men to wait for him in the yard.

He put a hand on Marcy's trembling shoulder. "Don't untie him, no matter what he says. Not until I get back."

He started for the door and she caught his sleeve. "Rim, what are you going to do?"

"You can guess."

"Rim, please use the law. Don't do it yourself. See the sheriff."

"The sheriff is on Ward's side of the fence."

"Give him a chance to prove it then. Please, Rim, for me."

"All right," he reluctantly agreed. Rim went out. He told five men to stay here to guard the place. He looked toward the shed beyond the bunkhouse where the bodies of Willie Temple and the others had been taken. First Rim intended to ride to the scene of the massacre. Even though it was now dark he might be able to see some sign. He brought along a bulls-eye lantern. The men rode quietly. There was the sawing of leathers, the faint metallic chiming of bit chains. A horse neighed.

One of the men kept rubbing the palm of his hand along the butt of his booted rifle. "Willie was a loudmouth. But I reckon he wasn't so bad."

"Yeah," Rim said heavily. "You like a man or not, if he's on your side of the fence and he's killed, you go looking for those who did it."

"Rim, you reckon it was Eric Ward's doings?"

"Who else?" Rim looked around at the dark file of riders behind him. "We may have some hanging to do if the sheriff gives us trouble. If we do, we'll use a double rope on Jellick. I don't want him coming down once we've got him swinging."

"How about usin' a twisted copper wire? I heard of 'em hangin' a fella that way over to Tascosa. They caught him with another fella's wife. Powerful sad way to die, so they tell me."

Rim looked around at the man who had spoken, trying to gauge the statement. But he decided, after a moment, that the rider had meant no reference to himself and Marcy Stallart.

As he faced around again, the night wind in his face, he wondered if he was a fool to play the game Marcy's way. Every instinct told him to go after Ward and Jellick. But he knew that other men would die if he did. Did he owe it to his crew to try and protect their lives? Or was there any protecting from men like Ward and Jellick? Could an inept sheriff keep the rangeland from being raked by gunfire?

Well, he had promised Marcy. He would try it her way. But only up to a point. Personally he felt that in the end it would be a gun in his own hand that would settle the thing. If it was ever to be settled.

Later, they looked down on the lights of LaVentana.

CHAPTER TEN

Sheriff Jared Dort was just unloading a tub of clay he had dug along the river when he heard the riders. He was at a shed behind the jail where he kept some of his tools. The moon was very bright above the Mogollon Rim in the distance. The sheriff had a lantern set on the ground at the tailgate of his wagon. He staggered into the shed with the heavy tub, set it down and wiped his brow. When he came out he saw that there was a large body of horsemen in front of the jail. And so large a body of men as this, hours after supper time, had attracted a curious crowd of townspeople. The sheriff could hear voices, shouted questions. But none of the riders seemed in a mood for answering.

Straightening his back from the strain of carrying the tub, the sheriff went around to the front of the jail.

"From the looks of this," Sheriff Dort said to the assemblage, "you'd think President Grant was down at the hotel passing out cigars. What's it all about?" Then he recognized Rim Bolden. Sheriff Dort said sarcastically, "Don't tell me you've found the tracks of a big man and a big horse again." He looked around at the others, expecting someone to join in his short laughter. Nobody did.

Rim Bolden said, "We've got five dead men out at Anchor, and one wounded."

Sheriff Dort had been rubbing a forefinger where a slat of the tub had pinched it. Now he slowly dropped his hands to his sides. "A shooting? What about?"

"Rustled cows. My boys went after them. From the looks of it they rode into an ambush."

This talk of five dead men was like a dash of ice water in the face. "Any idea who did it?" Dort asked.

"There were six men." Rim leaned over the horn, peering down at the sheriff. "One of them was big and rode a big horse. But I already told you that. Not that it'll do any good."

"I can do without your insolent tongue," Sheriff Jared Dort snapped. He felt his stomach coiling with tension. He wished he'd taken time to go over to the hotel and eat his evening meal before going to the river for that tub of clay. Excitement on an empty stomach gave him a sickness, and he imagined he could taste his liver. "You say there was one wounded?"

"Bert Stallart."

"What does he say about it?"

The sheriff noticed that Rim hesitated for a moment before saying, "Stallart's pretty badly shot up. He hasn't said much."

Dort regarded this Texan in the darkness. And he could think of other Texans, drunks, wearing their dirty gray uniforms, catching a kid. Roughing this kid up. This kid who had escaped from a Union stockade, wearing a suit of stolen clothing. A kid who told these crazy drunk Texans that he was South like they were. That he was trying to get back to his own outfit. And these goddam Texans, like this Rim Bolden here; they took that kid and they put a rope around his neck and tied the other end of the rope around a tie on a railroad trestle. And then two of them got the kid, each by an arm. They dangled him, hooting. And finally they let him fall. A woman in a farm adjoining the railroad track saw it all. She told Dort about it after the war was all done.

Sheriff Dort tried to fight down the animosity he felt for this man. After all, a sheriff was supposed to be impartial. Just because a man had come here from Texas was no sign he should be treated any different than anyone else. At least Dort tried to tell himself this, but without much conviction.

"You reckon Stallart will be able to talk by mornin'?" Dort asked.

"You don't have to talk to Stallart," Rim Bolden said. "You can ride out with me and see the sign. You can follow the sign left by the rustlers and the beef they stole. I suppose you have an idea where the tracks lead."

The sarcasm in Bolden's voice threatened to remove the checkrein from the sheriff's temper. "You tell me where the tracks lead," he said, and wished in that moment he'd kept his mouth shut.

"To Eric Ward's T," Rim Bolden said. There was a sudden quiet along the street. The mounts of the riders shifted their feet, neighed.

Rim Bolden said to the sheriff, "Are you riding out with us to see Ward? Or do we go alone?"

The sheriff stopped, picked up a stick, broke it in two. It made a snapping sound. He closed his eyes. It was the way the woman said his brother's neck had sounded when he was dropped off the trestle.

"I'm the law here," Dort said. "I'll investigate. You Anchor men get on home."

"How long will this—investigation—take?"

"You'll hear from me. I'll ride out to see you after I've talked with Ward." The sheriff started away, then looked around. "I'll be interested in hearing what Bert Stallart has to say about all this."

Rim Bolden sat his saddle, a big shadow, peering down at Dort. He said nothing for a moment, then, "All right, boys. We'll let the sheriff handle it his way. For now."

The Anchor men rode away into the darkness. Dort stood looking after them, thoughtfully rubbing his jaw. Making up his mind quickly Dort locked his shed, got his horse and rode in the direction of T.

Later, as he climbed the steep trail to Ward's yard, he was challenged. He identified himself and a man with a rifle told him to go ahead. As Dort rode past the guard he recognized the man as Tut Tyler, who used to work for Anchor.

At last he was in the yard of Eric Ward's sorry-looking outfit. It wasn't much better as a headquarters than the place Bert Stallart used as a horse camp.

The house door opened, thrust a fan of light into the yard. Ward said, "Who is it?"

"Me," Dort said, and dismounted.

"Come in, come in. Since when did you take to riding the night trails?"

Dort stomped dust off his boots and entered the house. At that moment another rider came into the yard and Sheriff Dort looked back over his shoulder. He saw the towering Meade Jellick slip from the saddle and enter the house.

Dort said, "Hi, Meade." He rubbed his hands together. "A little whisky and water might settle my stomach, Eric."

"Sure." Ward had been regarding him strangely. Now he went to a shelf and took down a bottle and some glasses. Ward filled three shot glasses. Jellick ambled over to the table. He picked up his glass in a big fist and downed the drink. The sheriff helped himself to a tin cup, poured the whisky into it then put in some water from a canteen hanging from a nail. He took a generous drink and the warmth seemed to uncoil the ugly tension in his stomach.

"Boys, I accepted your version of Simpson's death the other day," Sheriff Dort said. "That it was probably just a ruckus between two cowhands over a woman, maybe."

"I know you did," Ward said. His handsome face looked puzzled. He wore a new wool shirt, dark wool pants and half boots. "Has there been more trouble?" and his gaze slipped to Jellick, then back to the sheriff.

"Five men dead, one wounded. Anchor men."

Ward whistled softly. "Trouble between Stallart and Rim Bolden?"

Dort lowered his cup. "Why should there be trouble between those partners?" he asked slowly.

"Mrs. Stallart is a good-lookin' female," Jellick put in.

It took Dort a moment to mull this over. He decided to take a middle course. "I'll admit Bolden didn't seem to be telling a straight story when he brought Stallart's name into it. I got the feeling he was hiding something."

"Obvious. In country like this nobody likes to admit he's after another man's wife." And Ward added hastily, "Not that there's any reciprocation on Mrs. Stallart's part. Of that I am certain."

Dort finished his whisky, wondering just why Ward was so sure this was a fact. "Eric, you and me are doing a little business together. Nothing illegal from my point of view." Then he added, "Even so, I can't take sides."

"We stand to make a little money."

"I hate Rim Bolden's guts, but—"

"I've sensed that." Ward seemed to be waiting for him to explain this hatred, but the sheriff couldn't bring himself to do this. Just thinking about that kid the dirty bastardly Texans had accused of being a spy had drained him for one night.

Dort gave Ward a searching look. "I'd like to believe that this shooting was on account of Stallart and Bolden busting caps over Mrs. Stallart. And maybe dragging some of the Anchor hands into it. But I got to be sure, Eric."

Eric Ward was sitting on the edge of the heavy plank table. "Meade, have you had any trouble with the Anchor crowd?"

Jellick licked at the palm of his hand, held it over the chimney of the lamp on the table. He withdrew it quickly and studied the redness there on the palm. "I ain't had a chance to tell you, Eric. But some of the Anchor boys jumped us." He gave the details.

Sheriff Dort saw that Ward seemed surprised to learn this. Dort felt his own face slowly freeze as he faced Jellick. "Rim Bolden claims he was hit by rustlers."

"Bolden is a liar," Jellick said.

"Then you weren't driving Anchor cows?"

"Sure we was," Jellick said with a shrug of his tough shoulders.

Eric Ward slammed a fist on the table knocking the sheriff's cup to the floor. It struck with a clatter and rolled under the table. "Goddam it, Meade, why didn't you tell me about this?"

"I just got here for one thing. Took time to get them cows settled down. Besides, I didn't know how many Anchor men was down. They jumped us. We started shootin' and got out fast."

"What were you doing with Anchor cows?" Sheriff Dort demanded coldly.

"Bought 'em." Jellick gave a tight grin. He took a paper from his pocket and handed it to the sheriff.

Dort could not conceal his surprise. It was truly a bill-of-sale for two hundred head of Anchor beef. It was dated this day and signed by Bert Stallart. Frowning, he put the paper on the table. He was wondering why Rim Bolden's name as partner wasn't on that document. But, he reasoned, Bolden only had a small interest in Anchor. He supposed Bert Stallart could do just about as he pleased.

"Obviously Stallart and Bolden are trying to cover up a jealous fight," Ward said, "by blaming me."

"But Jellick said they jumped him. Why?"

"Ask Stallart," Jellick said.

"I aim to," Sheriff Dort said. He rubbed his jaw. There was clay under his fingernails. He picked some of it out. It was a long minute before he spoke. "I got my personal likes and dislikes in this country, Eric. But after all I'm the sheriff. I wangled a beef contract for you from my brother and—"

"And you get a cut of it."

"That's all right so far as it goes. But I want to warn you boys. I'll come after you quick as I will after Bolden or Stallart if I got to."

Ward's eyes held a faint edge of anger. "That's a pretty thin speech. I think if it came to a showdown my word would have a little more weight when it came to keeping you in office. More weight than Anchor's, for instance."

And Dort, thinking it over, had to admit this was probably true. Even though Ward had only been in this area a comparatively short time he was well-liked.

"One thing I can't figure," Sheriff Dort said. "Just why would Bert Stallart be sellin' you beef now?"

"Some money he owed me," Ward said easily.

"For how long?" Dort wanted to know.

Ward glanced at Jellick, then said to the sheriff, "He's owed the money since he lived in Kansas."

"Funny, but you never said anything before about knowing him in Kansas."

"I didn't think it was important." Ward let a smile flicker across his Ups. "I get along with Stallart fine. It's his partner who balks at Stallart paying his just debts."

Sheriff Dort looked thoughtful. "Well, like you already know, I got no feelin' for Rim Bolden. But—" He cleared his throat. "How come Stallart pays you in beef now? Why not after roundup?"

"I asked for payment now. I don't have enough cattle in my own brand to warrant holding a roundup. I want to start building a herd and I feel that Stallart might as well start paying me off now instead of later."

"You mean he owes you more than two hundred head?" The sheriff said, shaking his head.

"It was a sizeable debt." Ward spread his hands. "Let's not worry about that. All we want is some beef to trail to Fort Slaughter."

"Yeah, reckon."

Ward said, "You'd better spend the night here. It's a long ride back to town."

"I got some thinkin' to do, Eric. My brain works better when I'm to home."

* * * *

When the sheriff had ridden down the slope on the town road Ward turned on Jellick. "Might be a good idea, from here on out, if you let me know just what in hell is going on."

"I just saw me a chance to cut down the opposition a little. I took it."

"But Mrs. Stallart's brother. My God, that's going to hit her hard."

"I done you a good turn, Eric," Jellick said. "The kid favored Rim Bolden for a brother-in-law. He said it often enough."

"I just wish it would have been possible to leave Marcy Stallart out of it altogether."

"You told me yourself we got our ropes on a prime bit of money here. Why get our wagon mired down in the gumbo over some female? You'll get her, sooner or later."

"You're damned quick to shoot off that gun of yours," Ward snapped. "But I notice you haven't done anything about Rim Bolden yet."

"I will."

"It better be soon. We don't have to worry about Bert Stallart giving us trouble with our *estimable* Sheriff. But we've got a little worrying to do on the subject where Rim Bolden is concerned."

"The sheriff hates Bolden. He made it plain enough tonight."

"We can't bank our lives on that fact," Ward said. "Maybe Dort isn't much of a sheriff. But one thing I've learned about him. He has a conscience."

"Maybe we'd have been better to steer clear of Dort altogether."

"Probably. I thought he was hungry for some round Yankee dollars. But apparently not hungry enough to look the other way. We'll have to play it carefully from here on out."

"A little late, Eric," Jellick said. "When Bolden finds out the sheriff won't move in on us, he'll do it himself. There'll be some dead men around these parts."

"Yes, damn it."

"Well, it's what you wanted, ain't it?" Jellick demanded peevishly. "You wanted Bolden dead. When he comes pilin' up that trail with his men that's just how he'll be. Dead."

Jellick went outside and Ward poured himself a drink. Maybe he should send for April now. Have her come out and become acquainted with Marcy Stallart. Ward felt that his sister could pave the way for him with Marcy Stallart. April was a lady, that much was for certain. Her schooling had cost him enough.

He fell to thinking about the dark-eyed Marcy. He hoped fervently that when Rim Bolden was in his grave she wouldn't blame him, Could the entire blame for this bloody business be placed squarely on Meade Jellick's heavy shoulders? He closed his eyes and pictured himself paying a call on the bereaved Widow Stallart. Ward would tell her how much he regretted that her husband, Bert Stallart, was dead. But maybe it was better this way, he would say. Better for a man to be dead of a bullet, than by a hang rope—

And he would say, "I wanted to do this peacefully, Mrs. Stallart. It was Meade Jellick who went crazy and killed your husband and Rim Bolden. I don't believe in vengeance ordinarily, but I took care of Jellick myself. And with the sheriff's approval." He pictured Marcy Stallart's dark eyes filling with tears. She would give him her warm hand to shake after this first meeting. On the second visit he would escort her into the country in a rented buggy. He knew about these warm-blooded Southern women. She wouldn't be too long in widowhood before feeling the need of a man. Eric Ward promised himself that he alone would be available when this happened.

Jellick came in, the floor shaking under his weight. "You got a smile on your face. You got something figured out?"

"Yes. A good long life—for the two of us."

It wasn't often, Ward thought that night after he had gone to bed, that a man had a chance to acquire a ranch the size of Anchor. Or a woman as handsome as Marcy Stallart.

All the bad years of the war and those that followed could be forgotten if only he could succeed in this one thing. All the years of planning, of striving, of disappointments.

It had been the luckiest day of his life when he met up with a drifter named Meade Jellick, and one night heard the story of Bert Stallart. At last Ward knew what to do with the small stake he had acquired with his own brand of playing cards, coupled with his ability to out-shoot most men. He came to New Mexico and bought a broken-down ranch.

From his own bunk across the dark room, Meade Jellick said, "I'm gettin' a little edgy. Let's finish it up quick. Why drag it out at two hundred head of beef at a time?"

Ward pretended he was asleep—.

CHAPTER ELEVEN

The first visitor the next morning at Anchor was Doc Snider, who had returned from his semi-annual visit to Mesilla. It was no secret that he had a periodic fondness for quantities of frijoles, chili rellenos, chile verde, good bourbon whisky and the charms of a woman named Sanchez. This morning he made an elegant figure as he wheeled his buggy into the yard, tossed the reins to one of the men who tied his team. Doc Snider was a tall, angular man with a carefully trimmed graying mustache and goatee. His hand was damp and shook slightly as he offered it to Rim.

"Hear you have a patient out here," Doc Snider said.

"Bert Stallart." Rim led him to the house. "The cook made fresh tortillas this morning and there's a pot of frijoles on the stove—"

Doc Snider looked horrified. "God, no. Not that again. Not until September, at least. I've had my fill of—everything." He gave Rim a sly grin. "A man's weaknesses—Oh, well—What seems to be the trouble with our friend Stallart?"

"Gunshot wound. But not serious."

"Oh, yes, so the sheriff said. I've had a feeling about things in general around here. I guess that's why I took my trip to Mesilla earlier than usual this year. Has this shooting got something to do with Ward moving in as a neighbor?" And when Rim shrugged the doctor went on, "Just seemed odd that a man would set up a brand that was so easy to change from an Anchor. Almost as if he *wanted* to be accused of rustling. Everybody was surprised Stallart let him get away with it." Doc Snider's sharp blue eyes, a little bloodshot yet, studied Rim's dark face. "Or that you'd let Ward get away with it. Seeing that you're a partner in Anchor."

"I was on the range a lot when Ward moved in. I didn't know about it till he was already set."

They went into the kitchen and Rim asked the Mexican cook to fix steak and eggs for Doc.

"I hear Stallart's niece bore a son," Doc said. "Stallart had plans for the boy."

"Yes. Did you hear that in town?"

"His niece told me herself," Doc Snider admitted. "She's pretty bitter. Says Stallart kicked her out, you might say. She'd have gone away penniless if it hadn't been for some money Marcy gave her."

"It was a shock to Bert, all right. Having Ellamae arrive here about ready to drop her child."

Doc Snider spooned coarse brown sugar into his coffee. "When will humans stop making such a to-do about wedlock? Why not honor the institution of birth, no matter what the circumstances?"

"That's a long time in coming. If ever."

Rim leaned forward, telling Doc about the ugly rumors. How Stallart was tied in his bed upstairs.

"Sort of puts you in an awkward position, Rim. Being Bert's partner."

"After roundup I'm taking enough beef to cover my investment here and pulling out."

"I hope after roundup isn't too late. Maybe a smart man would leave now."

"Doc, you've got to understand something. I came out of the war with nothing but a broken-down Texas horse ranch. I spent a year rounding up my horses and breaking them. I managed to sell most of them as cavalry mounts at Fort Winthrop. I came up here with three thousand dollars. Stallart needed help because he was about finished here at Anchor. I liked him. I bought in." Rim started at his steaming cup of coffee before him on the table. "I'm within spitting distance of my thirtieth birthday. It's a little late for a man to start over. I can't just turn my back on everything."

"Funny how a man will put such a cheap value on his very life."

"Three thousand dollars or three hundred. It makes no difference, Doc. I've got a right to be here. Until I can clear out on my own terms I'm going to stay."

"You're a good man, Rim. If we'd had more like you on our side Lee might have been the dominant figure at Appomattox Courthouse."

"It was starvation that whipped us, not a lack of guts," Rim said fervently. "But I don't want to talk about the war. It's why I came up here. I thought there'd be a mixture here of North and South."

"There is."

"I wanted to live among my neighbors and forget that four year madness," Rim said.

Doc finished his coffee and the Mexican cook placed before him a platter of fried beef and eggs. He ate ravenously, pausing now and then with fork in the air to express an opinion. One of them concerned Ellamae's visit to him in LaVentana.

"I just got in last night and the first visitor I had was this girl. She accused me of being an old drunk. She said if I hadn't been in Mesilla her baby could have been saved. That I doubt, if the facts she related are correct. That baby was born with a face cold and blue as a winter sky. He had no chance whatsoever." Doc gave a weary shake of his gray head. "Of course the part about me being an old drunk is partially true. I guess every man living has some cross to bear. The weight of mine only becomes intolerable during those two periods of the year. But of course, I couldn't explain that to Ellamae Stallart."

"She should get out of New Mexico. Forget her bitterness toward Stallart."

"But she won't."

Doc looked around. "Where *is* Marcy this morning?"

"I imagine she's alone with her grief."

"Because Bert got himself shot?"

Rim looked at him. "You don't know about the rest of it?"

"Sheriff Dort said Bert was shot and to get out here first thing. For God's sake, don't tell me it's even worse than I supposed. And me sitting here—"

Rim told him about Willie and the four Anchor hands lying dead in the shed beyond the bunkhouse.

"Sweet Mother of God," Doc Snider breathed.

"We'll have the service soon as you take a look at Bert. Some of the boys are digging the graves now."

The doctor's face was gray. "But why has Bert let Ward push him into a position like this? Why?"

"I wish I knew. Ward and Meade Jellick are holding something over his head. Bert acts like a man who's scared gutless. I can't understand it at all."

"Most any other man and I might say it was possible to force him to do something against his will. But Bert Stallart—I just can't believe it."

There was the sound of a horse in the yard. Rim went to the window. Sheriff Jared Dort was just swinging down from a roan. The sheriff came purposefully to the kitchen door and knocked. Rim told him to come in.

The sheriff eyed him coldly, then said, "You patch Stallart up yet, Doc?"

"Looks as if Stallart is the least of the patching that should have been done," Doc Snider said from the table. "Why didn't you tell me about Mrs. Stallart's brother and the others?"

"Wasn't no use. Not unless on your last trip to Mesilla you learned how to bring the dead back to life."

Doc flushed at the reference to Mesilla. He got up. "If you'll lead the way, Rim."

"You'd better go alone, Doc," Rim said. "You know the way."

"I'll just go have myself a talk with Bert Stallart," the sheriff said. "Come along, Doc."

Rim said, "In that case, I'd better go with you two."

"You just set down there, Bolden," Sheriff Dort said coldly. *If* you don't mind."

They went out, the sheriff with his clay-stained fingers, the doctor carrying his bag, his steps a little shaky from his recent sojourn in the southern part of the territory.

Rim walked out into the bright sunshine to see how the grave-digging had progressed. He found the men sitting on the mounds of fresh earth, shovels laid aside.

"She's all ready, Rim," one of them said.

Rim picked up a handful of the cold earth, crumbled it in his fingers. It this all a man fights for all his life? he thought bitterly. Just so he can find himself a grave that in the passing of a decade, maybe even less, will be unmarked?

CHAPTER TWELVE

The service was brief. The coffins were lowered into the ground and covered with earth. The headboards Ed Rule had made that morning were put in place. Marcy wept quietly. She stood away from her husband. She did not look at him once. All during the service Rim was conscious of Bert Stallart's gaze on him.

When it was over Doc Snider got Rim aside. "Think over what I said," he warned gravely. "About a man putting a three thousand dollar value on his life."

"Good-by, Doc. Thanks for coming out."

Doc drove off and Marcy and Bert Stallart went into the house.

Sheriff Dort came over to where Rim stood, his eyes bleak. "I was almost beginning to think you were getting the muddy end of the stick around here, Bolden," Dort said. "That is until I heard what I did upstairs."

"Think the worst," Rim snapped. "You will anyway."

"Two partners and one woman between you. That's a pretty low way to go about getting yourself a ranch. And a woman!"

"Take that badge off, Dort," Rim said. "And I'll feed it to you a little at a time."

"There ain't a goddam Texan born of woman that puts the fear in me. Least of all you, Bolden."

"The hell with how you feel about me. But you're slandering a good woman."

"I wasn't sure about her. But I am now. She took your part. Against her own husband."

"She defends the truth against a lying tongue," Rim said. "Does that make her a wanton?"

"I want nothing more to do with you, Bolden. Jellick told me some things about you in town this morning. I didn't know whether to believe them. But I do now."

"Jellick—in town," Rim mused, but the sheriff had mounted and was riding out of the yard.

Ed Rule said, "Don't do it, Rim."

Rim turned around, surprised that the old cook had come up behind him. "Don't do what?"

"Go to town and tangle with Jellick. Not 'less you take some of the boys."

"Enough boys are dead already." Rim gave Rule a light tap on the arm with his fist. "You stay out of my business, old man."

"If you got to mess with Meade Jellick," Rule said seriously, "shoot him in the guts. Don't let him get a hand on you."

Rim touched the butt of his low-slung gun. "I'm not going to town to palaver with Jellick or Indian wrestle. I'm going to town to kill him."

Rim rode out, cutting into the hills away from the road. He didn't want to run into Doc Snider, whose buggy he could easily overtake. Most of all he didn't want to see Sheriff Dort. He'd had enough of the sheriff for one day.

* * * *

He approached the town from the south, coming in along Caballo Creek. He came upon the stage road from Mesilla and Paso and followed this for a mile. He was lost in dark and bitter thoughts when he caught sight of a yellow flower in the trees that bordered Caballo Creek, only a dozen yards from the road. Only it wasn't a flower. It was the yellow head of a woman. Ellamae Stallart, sitting on a blanket, her feet drawn up under her, was regarding him somberly. Rim drew rein, looked around. He saw a yellow-wheeled buggy in the trees. Saw a team of horses tied off.

He rode up and dismounted. "Hello, Ellamae," he said, his gaze searching the trees. "You here alone?"

"I'm with a fella."

"What fella?"

"None of your business." She had unpinned her long hair and now it hung loose about her shoulders. She wore a black dress with a frilly neckline. Her face was thinner than he remembered, paler. Her eyes were bitter.

"Where's this fella of yours?" Rim said, and looked toward the creek.

"Right here!" a heavy voice said from behind him.

Rim, half-turned, felt something strike him in the small of the back with such force that he was driven to his knees. Half-paralyzed, he saw the hand ax that had been hurled at his back, thankfully striking with the flat end instead of the bit. Pain blurred his vision but he was able to see the immense shadow pounding down on him. He saw an armload of firewood come spilling down. Then he felt his gun torn from its holster.

Meade Jellick said, "I go to cut wood for cookin'. Look what I find!"

Rim heard Ellamae say, "Leave him alone, Meade."

Jellick ignored her. "You got luck, Bolden. By rights you ought to be bleedin'. With half your back bone tore out. I need practice. I ain't throwed one of them things in a long time."

Desperately Rim tried to get his legs to work. He lay on his side. He began inching away but Jellick aimed a kick at his face. The swinging boot toe missed him by only half an inch as he drew back his head. The boot caught him in the shoulder. It knocked him hard against the ground. Jellick came for him again, grinning. This time Rim got to his knees. He swayed. Jellick came to stand over him, and he laughed.

"Ellamae, I brung you out here for a picnic. If seein' a man's brains layin' in the dust turns your stomach you better go on down to the creek."

"My God, Meade," she whispered, getting to her feet. "Don't kill him!"

Jellick leaned over to get Rim by an arm and drag him to his feet. But Rim came up of his own accord. He suddenly found strength in his legs. He bowed his head and the back of his neck came right up under Jellick's crotch. Rim heaved up, lifting Jellick off the ground. It was like carrying a young bull on your back. The shock of Jellick's big fists pounding his head and back almost drove him off balance. But he managed to take a few running steps. He launched himself in the air. As he fell he saw Jellick, arms flailing, catapult some half dozen yards away. Jellick fell with a crash on the side of his head. He lay huddled there like a wounded bear.

"I hope I broke his neck," Rim panted, and looked around for his revolver.

Ellamae stood as if frozen, seeming unable to speak.

But before Rim could find the gun Jellick had taken, he saw the big man come up suddenly and sprint toward him. Jellick's arms were wide from his big body, seeking to trap him in their circle.

Rim waited till Jellick could almost touch him with the tips of his fingers. Then he sprang aside. Jellick went past him like a runaway horse. And Rim's whipping fist struck Jellick's right ear so hard that it split the lobe. Jellick fell, skidding on his face. Instantly Rim was on him, getting the fingers of one hand in Jellick's greasy hair. Drawing the head back so the face was exposed. Smashing with his right into Jellick's face until the knuckles ached. And then Jellick, bellowing with pain, pretended to cover the wreckage of his face with a forearm. But the arm shot out, wrapped around Rim's knees, pulling Rim down. His weight pinned Rim flat on his back.

Jellick stranded him and Rim felt the bleeding from Jellick's face on his own. And Rim fought for one of Jellick's hands and caught the wrist that seemed big around as a wagon tongue. Jellick's other hand flashed to his throat and Rim tensed his muscles against the pressure. From a deep cavern of his mind came a roaring that grew. And with it came a redness and then black. It was his life that was swiftly melting into that blackness. And from some inner core he cried out for strength to lift this madman off of him and break the murderous fingers at his throat.

The only thing that saved him was the fact that Jellick only had one hand at his throat. If Rim had not managed to hang onto the other wrist the last life-giving breath would have been crushed out of him seconds ago.

But Rim suddenly released his hold on the wrist and clawed for the eyes. Never before in his life had he purposefully sought to blind a man. But he would have felt no guilt if he could have dug from the skull the eyeballs of this man who sought his death.

At the last moment Jellick jerked his head away and the clawing fingernails dug into flesh of cheek and jowl instead of eyesocket.

This shifting of Jellick's weight gave Rim a chance to gain leverage. He heaved up, but not enough. Jellick was leaning on him again, seeking his throat. But Rim, holding both of his hands together, drove them upward, breaking apart Jellick's grip. This he followed with a smashing blow to the jaw that snapped Jellick's head back. And Rim twisted his body, toppling Jellick.

There was a sudden sound from the road and Rim shifted his gaze and saw two men on a hay wagon, staring. They were trying to hold in their team that was jumpy from the scent of blood and the sight of two big men pounding one another.

"Holy Kee-ryst!" one of the men said, awed. "It's Jellick and Rim Bolden!" He grabbed a revolver from the floorboards of the wagon. Pointing it at the sky he emptied it. "Everybody ought to see this!"

The team, already skittish, nearly got away, but the second man held them in.

But Rim was only vaguely aware of all this. Jellick was coming for him again. He fought him off, took two crushing blows to the face. There was the salty, mineral taste of his own blood. He struck savagely at Jellick's midriff and was rewarded by a blast of stale beer breath that must have been lifted from deep in the man's stomach. But one of Jellick's wildly swinging fists caught him at the right temple. Rim's vision rocked. He groped, clung to the front of Jellick's shirt to keep his legs from going out from under him. Jellick's big yellow teeth snapped at his left ear. Rim jerked free, having a dim view of three Jellicks charging at him again. He lashed out and the three must have merged into one for he felt the man's solid jawbone under his knuckles.

It was hit and back up, hit and sidestep. With Jellick always pressing. Jellick using short jabs and swinging wide, his fists like rocks swung from leather thongs.

They grappled and Rim, his head on Jellick's heaving chest, felt a blinding pain at his crotch. He fell, but his hands caught at Jellick's belt. He toppled Jellick. They broke apart. And Rim managed to crab-crawl across the ground, Jellick trying to kick at his head every step.

And Rim, in that moment, knew that had Jellick's lifted knee struck solidly it would be over now. The pain subsided. Rim rolled away from Jellick's boots. But his back was momentarily turned. Jellick kicked him at the spot where the hurled ax had struck earlier. Rim screamed. For a moment he thought the paralysis would grip him again. But it didn't. On his knees he turned, meeting Jellick's rush. He caught a swinging leg just below the knee. He twisted, putting all his weight on it. If only he could shatter the bone—Jellick gave a great squeal of pain. He kicked like a trapped horse. Rim was knocked ten feet away. Rim got up shakily and he saw that Jellick's two legs were still solidly supporting the weight of this indestructible giant.

For the first time Rim felt a shadow of fear. He saw that the road and the area by the creek was packed with men who had come from town, a quarter mile away, drawn by the firing of the revolver by the teamster. He saw the staring faces, saw the eyes shining with excitement. And he knew that what they saw here today would be told as long as there was a campfire in these hills. Told and retold. And maybe with it set to music. With a cowhand and a banjo singing about the death of Rim Bolden. And a vaquero with a guitar, singing in Spanish of the futile fight of Señor Bolden. "Ah, you should have seen that day, compadre. The ground was red as if you opened a cask of wine and let it flow upon the soil. And those two. Ai—ai—ai—you would not recognize them as men. Their faces were masks of blood but you could see their eyes. The eyes hated—."

CHAPTER THIRTEEN

Jellick was bent over, gasping for breath. And for once Rim did not move in on him. His legs felt as if anvils were tied to his ankles. His arms were weighted as if cast in solid lengths of iron. He could hear his own breathing. It reminded him of spring wind howling in a rocky draw.

Allie Grindge, who owned the Jewel Saloon, was one of the spectators. He peered at the weary combatants through his steel-rimmed spectacles. "Boys, boys," he said. "Call it off. Call it off."

Jellick laughed and straightened up and came for Rim again. Rim struck him. Felt the knuckles of the big man rake his numbed face.

They circled, slugging. In close they used elbows and knees. The crowd was shouting. Horses reared, showing rolled eyes at the excitement. The stage coming from Mesilla had pulled up. Two of the passengers had alighted, a slim dark man in a black suit. And a girl with red hair who wore a pale green dress. She seemed gripped by some horrible fascination as she watched the fight.

The stage driver yelled, "Get in, get in! I can't hold this team much longer!"

But neither the girl nor the dark man heeded him. The stage drove off, the other passengers shouting their disappointment at not being able to see the finish.

And the end was not long in coming. From some hidden reservoir Rim gathered the last flicker of his strength. He told himself, This is the man who killed Willie. The man who shot Simpson in the face and killed the others. The man who is trying to blacken Marcy Stallart's good name. The man who is trying to wreck my life by what he holds over the head of Bert Stallart—

As Jellick came for him Rim did not sidestep. He drove his left fist into Jellick's solar plexus. And at the same time he whipped his right to the jaw. But Jellick did not go down. He came on, blundering, cursing, trying to maul, to maim, to kill. A growing panic touched Rim as he gave ground before the avalanche.

"Dear God," he breathed through his torn lips, "give me a gun!"

But there was no gun, only his fists. They wrestled across the clearing, once piling into Ellamae who had stood her ground, terror-stricken.

They got up, tore at each other. They fell against the wagon and the team kicked wildly.

As Jellick twisted away from the wagon his left side was exposed. Rim hit him at a point just below the heart. Jellick tried to cover up and Rim hit him again. A great roar swept through the air and Rim did not know then if it was the crowd or the clamor in his own brain.

He struck, struck. He could hardly lift his hands.

The roaring increased it engulfed him. And he felt hands on his arms and somebody pounding his back. Dazedly he looked around. Excited faces hemmed him in.

"You done it, Rim!" a man shouted. "You done it!"

"Done what?" was all Rim could say.

"Jellick is down!"

And he was. Rim saw him lying in the road dust. A trickle of blood from Jellick's smashed nose made a small scarlet trail down the slope of a wheel rut.

Rim groped wildly. "A gun. Somebody give me a gun. I'm going to kill him—"

"No," Allie Grindge said. "It'd be murder."

"The hell with that. He isn't fit—fit to live."

Suddenly the road rolled out from under him. A storm must have come up suddenly for he was floating through a black cloud. He was dimly aware of voices: "Take him to town." "Take Jellick, he's worse off." "We'll send Doc for Rim Bolden." "Let's go drink whisky and talk about this."

Later, Rim heard a girl's voice say, "Get back. I'll take care of him."

And then Rim was increasingly aware of something soft under the side of his head. He opened one aching eye and saw a large green button and then some soft green cloth. The button and the cloth moved in and out, in and out. For quite a few seconds he wondered about this, then decided it was made by someone inhaling, exhaling. He felt warmth under him and a scent of lilac. Then, as he turned his head he felt a woman's shape under his head. He looked up into a young face that watched him over the edge of a rounded shelf of bosom. The face was pale now. She had large gray eyes and thick lashes. And she kept running the tip of her tongue along her full lower lip.

"I'm so glad you're conscious," she said.

"I must be dead," he breathed. "They don't have faces like yours. Not in this world. I must be in the next one."

"You don't have any broken ribs," she said, blushing a little.

He turned his head again. He saw he was stretched out and his head was in the girl's lap. The crowd had gone.

The girl said, "I never saw such a fight. It was terrible. And I never saw a man with such strength as yours." Then the girl looked away and said, "Here she comes with the water."

Rim got to his feet and the girl followed him up, looking worried. She steadied him with a hand on his arm. Rim saw Ellamae Stallart coming from the creek with a pan of water.

"I found your gun," Ellamae said, and jerked her head toward the buggy. "I put it in the seat."

Rim limped over and found his revolver. He put it into his waistband. On the floorboards he saw a frying pan and some bread and steaks wrapped in newspaper.

"Looks like I ruined your picnic," Rim said tiredly.

Ellamae shrugged. "You better get out of the country, Rim."

He looked down at his bloodied clothing, the shirt half-torn from his torso, the knee ripped from his pants. He put his gaze on Ellamae. It hurt him to talk. "You started right at the bottom, with this new life of yours," he said. "With a man like Jellick."

Before Ellamae could say anything the other girl came up. She was not tall, yet she had the appearance of height. There was dust on the back of her dress where she had sat on the ground, cradling his head. She dipped a small lace handkerchief into the pan of water Ellamae was holding. Standing on tiptoe the girl gently bathed his face.

Rim said, "Sight of me must turn your stomach."

She shook her head and he could see the fiery red lights in it. "I lived in Missouri during the war. Many a night I held a lantern for my mother while she tended the wounded on our side."

"And which was your side?"

"The North, of course." She squeezed water from the handkerchief, washed it again. Water in the pan turned a muddy brown.

Rim felt the ache in his back start up again. It was a wonder Jellick's hand ax hadn't ruined his spine.

They staggered over to their horses and were heading for LaVentana when Doc Snider arrived in his buggy. The doctor, with his long gray hair, mustache and goatee, didn't look quite so grand today. He seemed harassed. He gave Rim a long look, grunted something, then began to give him a superficial patching up. The two girls looked on.

When he had finished Rim said, "You act like you wished Jellick had finished me."

"I warned you to get out, Rim. For your own sake. You didn't see fit to take my advice."

"How's Jellick? Crippled up, I hope."

"You couldn't kill him with a hayfork. He'll be up and around by tomorrow. If I know his type he'll come after you with a gun." The doctor closed his black bag. He looked at the redhead, then said quietly to Ellamae, "Who's she?"

Ellamae said, "She was on the stage. She got off to watch the fight." Ellamae had hitched up her team to the buggy. The girl in the green dress walked over and asked her for a lift to town.

But Rim put in quickly, "I wouldn't do that, miss. Ride with Doc Snider instead."

The girl gave Rim a puzzled look, then studied Ellamae closer. Ellamae said, laughing, "You be seen riding into town with me and you'll have no reputation."

The girl turned crimson. Doc said, "You seem almighty proud of what you've made of yourself, Ellamae."

Ellamae climbed into her buggy. "Uncle Bert made me this way." She looked around at Rim. "You thank him for it."

She drove off, dust whipping around the buggy wheels. There was a strange, embarrassed silence.

Doc Snider seemed thoughtful. "If I were you, Rim, I'd get some rest for a day or so. You've been very lucky so far."

"Roundup's no time for a foreman to rest." Rim helped the redhead into Doc Snider's buggy. "Thanks for giving me the moral support," he said. "One look at you and I was very glad to still be alive."

"You seemed so—so helpless. I just *had* to do what I could for you."

"You'll be staying in LaVentana?" Rim asked.

"For several weeks, at least. You probably know my brother. Eric Ward. My name is April."

Rim met Doc Snider's gaze, looked away. "Send me a bill for the patching job, Doc. Good-by, Miss Ward."

Rim climbed stiffly into the saddle, wondering if ever again he would be a whole man. As he rode away he thought of his luck this day. Good luck in being able to whip Jellick. Bad luck in finding that a girl who interested him greatly was the sister of his enemy.

He was only able to ride for a mile before exhaustion claimed him. Unsaddling his horse, he hobbled it then, gun in hand, lay down in the brush. When he awoke it was dark.

He rode for Anchor Bar, taking his time because each step of the horse jolted every inch of his battered frame. When he finally got home, Rim went to his quarters and lay down on his cot. Presently Ed Rule came with a quart of whisky. Rim drank half of it while the old cook sat in a chair, watching him.

At last Rule said, "How does Jellick look?"

"Worse than I do," Rim said.

"There ain't no doubt about it now, Rim. You'll have to kill him. He'll be worse'n a trap-caught puma with young'uns." When Rim said nothing, Ed Rule went on, "And before this bloody business is over you'll have to kill Eric Ward."

"Ed, this is one hell of a world," Rim said tiredly, thinking of the redheaded April Ward.

"It ain't the world, Rim. It's just us bastards on it."

Half-drunk on the whisky Ed Rule had brought, Rim at last fell asleep. In the morning he was so stiff and sore he could hardly get out of bed.

Because of the condition of his face Rim did not shave. It was a silent crew that finally arrived at roundup camp on the West Fork of the Gila River, Rim in the lead.

Across the river the Sabers crew was already hard at work. There was hanging in the air, the odor of burned hide. Rim heard the familiar squeals of calves, the hoot of bulls, the hoarse protests of cows momentarily deprived of offspring. Dust rose from the camp and there were the shouts of the men, the slam of half a ton of beef against the hard earth. Branding irons glowed as Rim rode over. The men working the branding fires turned their sweating faces in his direction. They stared.

And Rim knew that he was a sight. One side of his face was swollen, his right eye nearly closed. There was a deep cut above the left eye and he felt as if every tooth had been jarred loose by Jellick's fists.

He drew rein, momentarily contemplating the feverish excitement of the camp. He thought of the days when he would have found himself enjoying this frenetic but integral part of the beef business.

Ray Burroughs, owner of Sabers, got up from where he was "sanding the hide" of a brander for burning too deeply with an iron on the flank of a calf. He came over, a big man in stained clothing who walked with a limp.

He offered his hand when Rim swung down. "I heard about the fight," he said. "Also about the shooting. How did Mrs. Stallart take it about her brother?"

"Not easy," Rim said, and noticing the rancher seemed faintly embarrassed, went on, "What else have you heard, Ray?"

"The rest of it." Ray Burroughs turned, spat tobacco juice into the nearest branding fire, watched one of his men, rope spinning, bring down a big steer with a shattering crash.

Rim pushed a hand against his aching face. "Ray, we're a little late getting started on roundup, but we're ready now. You want to pair up, your boys with mine and we'll make a gather and—"

"Rim, if we have a ruckus here it's liable to set the herd to running. A man could lose his winter wages in the tallow they'll run off."

"Naturally I can't guarantee there won't be trouble," Rim said stiffly. "Maybe we'd better have separate camps."

Burroughs explored a corner of his mouth with a juicy morsel of tobacco. "You see, if Anchor and Eric Ward tangle over that shooting. Or if you and Stallart tangle over Mrs. Stallart—Damn it, Rim, a man runs risk enough in this country without tryin' to walk barefoot through a rattlesnake cave."

Rim took his men back across the river. He felt let down. He knew Burroughs only used a possible stampede as an excuse. Burroughs wanted to stay neutral in any violence that might be shaping up.

He told Ed Rule to set up the chuck wagon a good mile from Sabers. "Wouldn't do to have them breathe the same air," Rim said bitterly. But he really couldn't blame the Sabers owner for wanting to stay out of it.

By noon of the following day they had over a hundred head of Anchor Bar calves licking their fresh and itching brands. The herd grew in size at the holding grounds. Rim took several rides into the hills, with some of his men, looking for sign of Ward or Jellick. But all he saw were Sabers men who gave him a wide berth, probably on orders from Burroughs.

It was just as well that neither Ward nor Jellick apparently were coming to him. As soon as he felt roundup was progressing satisfactorily, he would pay them a visit. There was so much to settle. He had never found it easy to kill a man, even in the war. With Jellick it was another matter. But Eric Ward now presented a problem. Because whenever Rim thought of Ward these days he couldn't help but see the redheaded April in his mind's eye.

But sister or not, it was a thing that had to be done. By what he had done personally, and by turning loose a man like Jellick in this country Ward had forfeited all right to live.

CHAPTER FOURTEEN

On this morning Bert Stallart found his superficial flesh wound did not stiffen up as much. He could get around a little better. Doc Snider had patched up one wound, but there was nothing that could ease the pain of the other, deeper wound that was festering inside his body.

He stood in the big empty yard, rubbing the marks on his wrists made by the thongs Rim had used on him. Stallart had tried mightily to free himself from the bed and the narrow strips of leather had cut into his flesh. The places on his wrists still had not healed.

There were three men, "pensioners," left at the place to look after things while roundup was in progress. Each man, at Rim's order now wore a loaded revolver and had a rifle near enough to grab if strangers showed up.

Stallart had one of the men saddle a horse. Then, without a backward glance at his wife, who stood watching him from a window, he rode out.

He was thinking of the advice Sheriff Jared Dort had given him. Most times he didn't think Dort had brains enough to make chalk marks on a black hat. But he guessed this time Dort knew what he was talking about.

Stallart went on down the trail, this mild spring morning, past the horse camp where he had heard Willie make his brag about Marcy and Rim Bolden getting married—in the event Marcy became a widow. And from the way Willie had talked, this seemed to be a mere formality. Ever since he had married Marcy two years ago he had been irritated by Willie. But in the throes of the honeymoon atmosphere that prevailed at Anchor Bar for some weeks following the ceremony, he had insisted Willie come to live with them. "Won't do for Bert Stallart's brother-in-law to be cleanin' stalls at the livery."

He made Willie segundo, but in the space of a few days it became apparent that the younger man's talents, if any, lay elsewhere.

He was wondering what to do about getting a foreman when Rim Bolden came up the trail from Texas. Anchor Bar was too big for one man to run alone and Stallart could not have any confidence in Willie as a helper. Yet he didn't feel like replacing him as segundo. Even though

Marcy agreed that Willie had weaknesses, still it would hurt her. So he put up with her brother.

And it was then he heard that there was a stranger in LaVentana with some fresh money, who wanted to buy the small Waterman place over east. Stallart lost no time in contacting Rim Bolden. A man could do better with his money, Stallart said, by investing in a ranch the size of Anchor Bar.

The two men seemed to hit it off and Stallart said it made no mind to him that Rim had been captain in the West Texas Volunteers.

That night Rim rode out with Stallart to Anchor Bar. And now Stallart, on this bright spring day was remembering how Marcy had put out her hand when Rim was introduced. How they looked at each other and Marcy, flushing a little, said, "You'll have to forgive me, Bert. But seeing somebody from home—and Texas does seem almost next door—" She turned quickly away and wiped her eyes.

"My wife was born and raised in Natchez, Mr. Bolden," Stallart had explained. "They come up this way and she lost her folks at Paso Del Norte. They got their drinkin' water out of the wrong well. And this is my brother-in-law Willie."

Willie squared his shoulders. "Sure a pleasure, Captain Bolden, suh. Wish I could have had the honor of fighting under you."

"I'm sure you wouldn't have enjoyed it much, son."

"Son?" Willie had exclaimed. "I'm almost twenty."

Marcy helped in the kitchen that night to make the meal a memorable one. She was gay and laughed a lot during supper. And Bert Stallart remembered how he had felt left out of it. Most of the people they talked about he had never even heard of.

Thinking about Marcy and Rim Bolden made the blood run hot through his veins. He drew rein where the bodies of Willie and the other Anchor Bar men had been found. There were dark stains on the ground and rifle shells gleaming in the sun. He followed the tracks made by the two hundred head of beef until at last he came to Ward's headquarters.

When he saw Ward and Jellick come out of the house to see who approached, there was one shattered part of a second when he considered drawing his gun and killing them while he had the chance. But he knew he wasn't fast enough for one thing; and his left side had stiffened up during the ride. Besides, there might be some of Ward's men lurking in the long shed-like structure across the yard that was used as a bunkhouse.

"You favor the sheriff's suggestion?" Ward said.

Stallart sat his saddle, looking at the towering Meade Jellick, seeing the cuts on the face, the misshapen nose, the eyes slitted purple. Stallart had heard about the historic battle from Ed Rule. But he didn't believe it when Rule said Rim had whipped the bigger man. He believed it now and he felt a grudging admiration for Rim.

He wished now he'd had the guts to hang Jellick with his own rope when the man first arrived at Anchor. It would have saved so much trouble. But had he done that he might never have found out about Rim and Marcy— "You ready to ride to town?" Stallart said.

Ward nodded. Then he said, "By the way, this transaction we're discussing today has nothing to do with our other business. Our Kansas business."

Stallart felt a muscle twitch at a corner of his mouth. "Maybe I'm getting tired of running."

"That could be," Ward agreed. "I don't blame you. A man doesn't like to be pushed too far. A man also doesn't relish the prospect of an ignominious awful death. A public hanging."

Stallart looked away toward the towering Mogollon Rim and he thought, Even the goddam mountains remind me of him. Mogollon Rim. Rim Bolden.

Jellick said, "What you figure to do about gettin' yourself a new foreman?"

Stallart hung the dipper back on a nail. "I don't give much of a damn what happens to Rim Bolden."

"Wouldn't make no difference if you did care. The man that lays a hand on me is the man that dies quick."

They rode to town, the three of them, Jellick beside Stallart, Ward in the lead. They followed the wagon road for a mile, then cut into the hills.

"About the other day," Stallart said. "How did my men happen to get shot?"

"They opened up," Jellick said. "I'd have showed 'em the bill-of-sale for them cows. But we never had no chance. They throwed a powerful lot of lead before we cut 'em down."

"Any of your boys get hit?"

"We were just lucky, I guess."

Ward, looking back over his shoulder, frowned. He drew rein and let them get ahead of him. For the rest of the way to town Ward rode with Stallart in front of him.

At the bank next to the Mountain Store, Eric Ward drew three thousand dollars in gold from his account. Sheriff Jared Dort had seen the trio ride in and now he hurried over to the bank in time to be a witness to the transaction. Meade Jellick, a sly look in the purplish, slitted eyes, went out the back door of the bank and cut for the alley behind the Jewel Saloon.

Sheriff Dort, noticing this, wiped the moist palms of his hands on his clay-smeared trousers.

"You better get home for now, Bert," Sheriff Dort advised when they were standing on the porch in front of the bank. Stallart held a canvas sack containing the gold coins.

"I ain't in no hurry," Stallart said, wondering why the sheriff seemed nervous all of a sudden. "Nothin' to go home for."

"You've got the money. Now do what I suggested about your ranch. Don't ruin it all now."

"I feel the need of a drink. Come along. I'll buy."

When they stood in the Jewel with glasses in their hands, Sheriff Dort advised, "You'd best be heading back to Anchor. Get your affairs straightened up with Rim Bolden. At least that'll be one stone off your back."

Stallart said, "I hear my niece is still in town." Nobody said anything.

Stallart was drinking steadily now, thinking about Ellamae and not about any business with his foreman-partner. He was remembering many things that concerned his niece. He was in that moment remembering his brother Paul, Ellamae's father. And a quick shuddering horror enveloped him. He squeezed his eyes shut and felt the sting of tears. That was the trouble with whisky. It melted down your guts. It was like an acid that ate into that one secret corner of your mind where you stored those things you could not afford to examine too closely. The things that could send you dangerously near the abyss of madness.

"What's the matter, Bert?" the sheriff asked worriedly.

"I'm a man that can't drink whisky."

"You've done all right," Dort said, eyeing the half-empty bottle. "Not that I'm against hard drinkin', but—"

"Me and Doc Snider. At least he makes a business out of it a couple times a year. But I've always got my feet draggin' in a whisky vat. At least so it seems lately."

Ward came in then and said, "Buy you a drink, Stallart, to bind our deal."

Stallart looked around, seeing the dapper, smiling man who was slowly ruining his life. Suddenly he turned his back on Eric Ward and asked Allie Grindge, behind his own bar, for a piece of paper and a pen. When this was supplied Stallart cupped a hand around the paper and wrote laboriously:

Ellamae:
    I am sorry about what I done to you. Come to Anchor and I will give you one thousand dollars when I sell cows.
                                       Yr. Uncle Bert

Stallart folded the note, handed it across the bar to Allie Grindge. "See that Ellamae gets this," Stallart said.

Grindge looked unhappy. But before he could carry out Stallart's request, Meade Jellick came down the narrow stairway at the end of the bar. There was a hard glint in the pupils of Jellick's discolored eyes. He grinned at Bert Stallart. The rancher had lifted his shaggy head to stare. Eric Ward, standing on Stallart's right, had stiffened, also looking at Jellick, as if sensing what was to come. Sheriff Dort muttered an oath and turned to Stallart and started to say something. Tension was on his face and Stallart could see the sudden spreading stain of sweat across the front of the sheriffs shirt.

Jellick came up to Stallart and gave him a twisted smile and helped himself to the bottle. Allie Grindge, looking pale around the mouth, set out a fresh glass for Jellick. It became so still in the place that a woman's shaky laughter upstairs sounded almost as loud as a gunshot.

Jellick drained his glass, the thick muscles working in his throat. "Your niece is a fixture here."

Stallart said, his lips barely moving under the tangle of mustache, "You mean—"

And then Stallart's gaze caught sight of something on the stairway. A pale-haired girl in a gingham dress, the sleeves cut off to show her bare arms. The bottom of the dress cut high to show her knees. Around her waist was a wide leather belt studded with conchae.

Jellick leaned close, whispered, "It was me put the idea in her head, Stallart. How'd you like to sweat a little bit more than you have been?"

There was a sudden avalanche of sound in Bert Stallart's mind. His right hand shot out, gripping the neck of the whisky bottle. Jellick, half-turned to grin at Ellamae on the stairs, did not see Stallart's move. Stallart swung the bottle at Jellick's head. The bottle shattered, throwing whisky across Jellick's face. Only the whites of Jellick's eyes showed as he crumpled with a jarring crash to the floor.

It was a blow that would have smashed the skull of an ordinary man. But Jellick, in that moment of stunned silence, stirred, then sat up. Blood streamed down the side of his face, across the front of his whisky-soaked shirt.

"You'll never live to hang, Stallart!" Jellick cried, and started to get up.

Stallart, standing there with the neck of the smashed whisky bottle in his hand, seemed unable to move.

"They'll never get you back in Kansas now!" Jellick bellowed and got his hands under him, and lurched shakily to one knee.

Ward pushed himself between Jellick and the pale, sweating Stallart. "Shut up, Meade!" he cried at Jellick. "Shut your mouth!"

"I'll kill him—"

"You'll ruin everything!" Ward snapped. When he saw Jellick trying to get to his feet, Ward drew his gun and stepped behind the big man. He brought the long barrel down on Jellick's head. Jellick's head swiveled as if trying to see who had struck him down. But his eyes were already blank. He fell and this time he didn't move.

There was an audible exhalation of held breaths in the big shadowed room. A wedge of sunlight, spearing through a narrow side window, fell across Jellick's closed eyes.

Sheriff Dort turned and looked at Stallart. "What did he mean about a hanging, Bert?" he asked quietly.

But it was Eric Ward who cut in. "Jellick doesn't know what he says half the time when he's drunk." He laid a ten dollar gold piece on the bar. "Drinks on me." He holstered his gun and wiped his moist face with a blue bandanna.

The men came slowly to the bar, and Sheriff Dort, a thoughtful look in his eyes, poured a drink and turned to hand the glass to Stallart. But the rancher was gone. Through the windows they could see him mounting up, holding the sack of gold coins in one hand. He rode out of town on the Anchor Bar road.

Allie Grindge said in a shaking voice, "Somebody better fetch Doc Snider."

Sheriff Dort came back from the front windows where he had watched Stallart ride out. He looked down at Jellick, who was already beginning to stir. "How much can one man take? Rim Bolden beat him up. And now he's had a whisky bottle and a gun laid across his skull—"

Eric Ward said quickly, looking around, "I'd appreciate it if you boys didn't tell Jellick that I'm the one who hit him that second time."

CHAPTER FIFTEEN

Last night Ed Rule had left roundup camp to return to Anchor headquarters for additional supplies. It was shortly before noon that he arrived back in camp, driving a buck board. Rim was helping some of the men haze down a dozen or so fractious cows from a thicket where they had taken sanctuary when he saw the old cook standing up in the wagon, waving his hat to get attention.

Rim spurred ahead, feeling apprehension tighten in him. "What is it, Ed?" he demanded when he reached the wagon with its foam-flecked team.

"It's Mrs. Stallart. I'm scared of what she—she might do to herself."

Rim felt a catch in his throat. "You mean—suicide?" It was incredible, Rim thought, that such a thing should even be uttered in connection with Marcy. She always seemed so poised, so filled with an inner strength.

"—Bert left early this mornin'," Rule was saying. "Don't know where he was headin' for. Mrs. Stallart sent the cook to town and locked herself in the house. I tried to get in the kitchen to get an extra sack of flour we need out here. But she wouldn't let me in. I peeked through the kitchen window. She was settin' at the big table with one of Bert's guns in front of her. She just sat there starin' at it."

"Why in hell's name didn't you stay there, Ed?" Rim demanded, concern for Marcy a flame in him now.

"What could I do. I asked her to let me in. She told me to go away, that she would be all right. But I didn't like the way she sat lookin' at that gun. Scared hell out of me. I told them three hands left at the place to keep their eyes open." Rule looked around. "I figured maybe Bert was out here—"

Rim had spent the morning on an Apaloosa, cutting cows out of the hills, bringing in some from the high reaches of the Mogollons. The horse was jaded. Quickly he shifted his saddle to a dun and rode out.

He took a shorter, steeper trail to Anchor headquarters, pushing the horse. His heart was pounding, and at each lunge of the mount he silently cursed Bert Stallart.

When at last he came to the ranchyard he saw the three "pensioners" in front of the bunkhouse, looking worried. Rim leaped from the saddle, looked toward the house. The kitchen door stood open.

"Where's Mrs. Stallart?" he demanded.

"Gone yonderly," one of the old men said. "Toward the Rock, likely. Leastways that's the way she headed."

Rim swallowed his anger. "Why didn't you go with her?" he demanded.

The men exchanged nervous glances. The spokesman spat through his gray beard. "We tried to, Rim, honest to Gawd. But she told us to stay put."

"Damn it, you could have trailed along."

"She's the boss' wife. We're only cowhands, Rim. It'd be like a rifleman tryin' to tell the colonel's wife what she oughta do. You just can't do it."

"How long has she been gone?"

"Most half an hour."

Rim took another horse, rode out, sweating. The Rock was a sandstone spire some four miles to the north. It had once been an Indian lookout post. It was high and it was a place where a person contemplating self-destruction could leap. The thought put a twisting agony through him—

He found her sitting high above on a shelf of the Rock. Her horse was tied to a stump at the bottom of the spire. She wore a boy's shirt and denim pants and boots. At the sound of his approach she looked around.

He left his mount beside hers and climbed the steep path to the shelf where she sat. "Hello, Rim," she said in a dead voice.

He stood there, rolling a cigarette. His fingers trembled. The paper broke under his clumsiness. He threw it away and watched the air currents sweeping through the deep canyon below catch up the piece of balled paper. He stared out at the vast wilderness, seeing the green of aspen and the deeper color of pines and junipers. There was a stillness that made a man feel insignificant; made his problems seem so unimportant.

"I like to ruined two good horses getting to you, Marcy," he said, and looked down at the dark head with its clean white part.

"You're the only one, it seems, who cares what happens to me."

"I was worried about you."

She turned her head and looked up, her dark eyes studying him. "You mean worried that I'd take my own life?"

"I did consider it, Rim," she went on and looked out across the hundred miles of rugged forested mountains. "Willie's death—and everything else—" She picked up a twig and broke it. "But you're right. When it came right down to the act I was revolted at such a sign of weakness in myself."

"Where's it going to end, Marcy?"

"Have you seen Bert yet?"

"No," he said roughly, and wanted to add that he didn't care much if he *ever* laid eyes on him again.

"Bert has a plan," she said. "He told me last night that Sheriff Dort suggested he borrow money from Eric Ward. And with the money buy out your interest in Anchor Bar."

"Going to Ward is like trying to offer beefsteak to the she-bear that has you pinned in her cave. Ward is Bert's enemy."

"I know," she sighed.

"You mean Bert will do anything to dissolve our partnership."

"I tried my best to make him understand the truth about—us. You and me, Rim. But he wouldn't listen. I feel there still is a lot of good in Bert—"

"That I'm beginning to doubt."

"—but how can he believe a man like Meade Jellick? He knows what Jellick is and yet Bert will say that Jellick saw you at the house, or Jellick saw us in a wagon together, or riding together."

"If Bert was my age I'd thrash him."

"There *is* a lot of good in Bert," she said again. "But he's suffering because of some past mistake."

"I've guessed that. But what mistake is it?"

She shook her head. "He refuses to discuss it."

Rim was silent a moment, watching a hawk, its dark wings rigid, ride the air currents out of the deep canyon.

Marcy said, "Are you going to accept Bert's offer to buy you out?"

"Do you want me to?"

"Yes."

"I planned to wait until after roundup, but—" He picked up a handful of gravel and felt it grind into his fingers as he clenched the fist he had bruised on Meade Jellick. "I suppose with me gone it would make things easier for you."

They rode back to the house together. And at the kitchen door Rim said, "Are you all right now?"

"I'll be fine. I guess it's facing one crisis that gives us strength for the next one. Good-by, Rim. You deserve the good things of this world. I hope you find them."

When he got back to roundup camp Bert Stallart was waiting for him. Stallart sat on an upended keg of horseshoe nails. He had a bottle. His eyes were red-streaked, glittering.

When Rim dismounted Stallart tossed a heavy sack at his feet. "Three thousand," Stallart said. "It's what you put into Anchor. There ain't no interest to go with it, but maybe you took the interest in other ways."

A quick rage flushed through Rim and he wanted to smash Stallart in the face. But he knew what must be done. For his sake, for Marcy's, he had to get out.

"I'm doing this for only one reason, Bert." Rim said, and the men crowding up, looked on tensely. "If I don't go I'll have to take a gun to you. I don't want that. For even as much as you've changed I remember that once you were a man I could like."

Stallart reacted as if he had been quirted across the face. For a moment he glared, then his eyes went dead. "I figured you'd cuss me. I never figured you'd say that." He took a long pull at the bottle.

Rim picked up the heavy sack, loosened the draw strings, saw the gold coins. He didn't count them. He drew the strings tight again. He wanted to get out of New Mexico, fast. "You've got a paper for me to sign?"

Stallart's voice shook when he said, "There's a paper at the bank. Sign it there if you're a mind to."

Rim said, "I came to Anchor with three horses. I'll rope out three before I go. I'll want a bill-of-sale, Bert. I don't figure to have somebody's rope around my neck for horse stealing."

"You must think I'm almighty low."

"You can answer that for yourself." Rim pulled his saddle, and walked down to where the hundred-head remuda was held in a rope corral. His practiced eye ran over the horses bunched there and he began to make his selections.

On his way out of this country he'd face up to Meade Jellick and Ward. He would do it for Marcy, not for Bert Stallart.

Then he thought of Ward's sister, April. It was the first time her image had crossed his mind in many hours. Was that the reason he had fought against going away with Marcy? Was it because of this redheaded girl he had only met once?

But he would bring her much sorrow, and how could there be any feeling at all in such a circumstance. She would always remember Rim Bolden as the man who killed her brother.

CHAPTER SIXTEEN

Rim Bolden roped out his first horse and saw Stallart ride up to some of the men who were standing around uncertainly. "Get to work!" Stallart shouted. "I ain't payin' you to count the wrinkles in your boots!"

Ed Rule, standing in the group of men, said, "You ain't much of a man to tie to these days, Bert. If Rim goes, I go."

"Rim's already gone, so far as I'm concerned," Stallart said. "I bought him out."

"You drove him out."

"Watch your tongue, old man!" Stallart said. "Or I'll fry it for breakfast."

Ed Rule just looked at him, and made a great show of removing his dirty apron and hanging it over the tailgate of the chuckwagon. "You've done turned against everybody, Bert. You turned against your partner. You turned against your wife!"

"My *wife!*" Stallart said, his lips twisting.

"You believing men like Jellick and Eric Ward. Believing them instead of trusting the people who are on your side of the fence. Who *were* on your side of the fence," Ed Rule corrected.

Stallart seemed to be having an inner struggle. "Damn it, Ed, don't quit on me in the middle of roundup."

"Then ask Rim to stay."

"I'll see hell's door froze shut before I'll do that!"

"You might see hell a lot closer than the door, Bert," Ed Rule said. "Before this thing is finished off."

"If that's how you feel," Stallart said, his voice breaking, "get out!" He neck-reined his horse, facing the men grouped around the branding fires who were silently watching. "How many of you boys are stickin' with me? Let me count hands."

Most of them signaled their intention of staying. Rim, watching from the edge of the rope corral, knew it was because jobs were so hard come by. He could see, however, that none of them seemed particularly joyous to be staying with Anchor. Ed Rule and six others made ready to quit the camp.

"Let's get them cows down outa the hills," Stallart said to the others. "Come on, boys. Spread out. Each man bring in six head if he can."

Stallart galloped past Rim without looking at him. It seemed to Rim that Stallart's face was jerking, and he appeared close to tears. Although even the thought of a tough rancher like Bert Stallart shedding tears for anything at all seemed ridiculous. And yet—

Rim started to saddle one of the horses he had chosen. He wanted that bill-of-sale for three head of horses. He intended to get it.

By the time he got the horse saddled Stallart was out of sight, but Rim had seen which way he had gone. He cut for the timbered hills, following Stallart's tracks. He passed some of the Anchor hands chousing cattle down to the holding grounds. These men lifted their hands to him, not yet knowing that he was through at Anchor. He didn't bother to tell them. All he wanted was that bill-of-sale out of Stallart. Then he'd push on.

Maybe with him gone Stallart would be able to clear the fog of jealousy from his mind and make a semblance of a life with Marcy, at least. But it was out of Rim's hands now. At least he had his three thousand dollars which he had spread out in his saddlebags, so as to distribute the weight. It was a lot more money than most men had these days.

The payment in money was something he could thank Stallart for, no mistake about that. No matter how the man had acted these past weeks. Had Stallart been a different type, Rim knew full well, the payment might have been a rifle bullet between the shoulder blades.

Rim was so engrossed in his own thoughts that as his horse climbed through the junipers, he came suddenly upon three riders some distance ahead. The size of one of them alerted him instantly, for although they were a hundred yards away or more, half-screened by brush, he easily recognized Meade Jellick. The big man wore no hat. There was a dirty bandage around his head. One of the men with Jellick was Tut Tyler, the Anchor hand Rim had fired. All Rim could see of the other man was a thick brown beard. He didn't know him. The three men were sitting their saddles, peering downslope at something that evidently moved below.

So suddenly had they appeared within his range of vision, that Rim had no time to seek cover. But they had not spotted him yet. He was downwind from their mounts, and sounds of his approach had been drowned out by a stream that roared down through a flume of rock just behind them.

As Rim jerked free his booted rifle Jellick rose high in the stirrups. Rim saw sunlight flash on the barrel of Jellick's rifle. But it wasn't pointed at him. Jellick began firing on someone below.

Rim heard Bert Stallart's faint cry, "Jellick—no!"

"Pay for my busted head!" Jellick shouted.

Rim's first shot went wild because the brown-bearded man had seen him and fired. A shudder wracked Rim's horse. And he knew that he had no chance unless he could seek cover. All he could do now was kick free of the stirrups, for the horse was pitching forward on its nose. Rim struck the ground on a shoulder that had been bruised in his fight with Jellick. He felt a flash of pain. A bullet struck the ground a yard in front of him. Instinctively he closed his eyes, but even so a great gout of dirt nearly blinded him. He rolled aside and felt the lethal brush of a bullet so close to his face that it froze him. All three of them were shooting at him now.

But he managed to cradle his rifle, and he squeezed off a shot at Jellick. But at that moment Tut Tyler wheeled in close on a dun. The bullet struck him with such force that it knocked him backward out of the saddle. And Jellick was forced to rein in to keep from being struck by the falling body.

Rim came to one knee, firing. He felt the ground jar under him again, rock chips stung the back of his hands. Ahead the horses of Jellick and the brown-bearded man reared, broke apart. Tut Tyler's mount went crashing off into the brush. Again Rim tried for Jellick, but the big man had neck-reined his roan to send it leaping the stream and Rim guessed the reason. Far behind him he could hear the shouts of Anchor men, coming on the run, drawn by the firing.

But the brown-bearded man twisted in the saddle for a final shot. And Rim's finger was already pressing the trigger. The beard was suddenly bright with color as a pumping stream of redness came from a bullet hole in the throat.

The man fell loosely and before Rim could lever in another shot Jellick was out of sight beyond a shoulder of rock.

Five Anchor men came pounding up the trail and Rim shouted, pointing in the direction taken by the T rider: "Jellick! Get him!"

The men thundered past Rim, drawing in a bit to look at the pair on the ground, then they went on. Rim picked himself up, shaky in the knees. He looked at his dead horse, seeing the bulge of the saddlebags that held his three thousand dollars. Just sheer luck that he still lived to count it.

He could see the loose horses of the two T men deep in the aspens ahead, but they were too far to catch. He turned his back on the gold-filled saddlebags, and hiked up the trail. There were other things more important than money now.

He came first to the brown-bearded man, laying face down in a great rust-colored pool of dust. Fifteen yards higher on the slope he came to

Tut Tyler crumpled on his side. A wedge of dark color stained the front of his shirt.

"Rim," he gasped, and coughed. "I never figured it to be no ambush. I—"

Rim turned him over on his back, trying not to feel anything for this man he knew would be dead within the hour. "You chose your side of the fence, Tut."

"Jellick said he just wanted to see how Anchor—" Tyler coughed again. This time his lips were stained as was the front of his shirt. "Honest to Gawd, Rim, I never figured he'd try and 'bush Stallart—"

Rim drew Tyler's belt gun, threw it into the brush. He kicked aside the man's rifle.

"It was my damn luck, Rim," Tyler gasped, "that I run into Jellick today. If I'd delivered the message like I was supposed to—"

"What message?"

"Some gal stayin' at the hotel in town. Said she was Ward's sister. Wanted me to ride out and tell him she was waitin' for him. But I went to the Jewel. I got drunk. And then when I sobered up I seen Jellick and—"

Rim got up and peered downslope but the junipers were so thick here he couldn't see Stallart. He started away, but Tyler said, frightened, "Get me to the doc, Rim. I—I got a chance if you get me to the doc."

Rim looked back at him. He thought of the evenings at Anchor when he had sat across the table from this man with nothing more deadly between them than a stack of poker chips. It sickened him to see the fear in Tyler's eyes. How would it be when his own time came? Was the fear of dying in every man?

The riders who had gone after Jellick now came streaming back to report they had lost his trail.

"Got clean away," the youthful Charlie Daws said.

Tom Niles, the scar on his swarthy cheek livid, said, "That Jellick is harder to catch than a black rabbit at midnight. He got away just like he done when he got Simpson."

"Give me a horse, somebody," Rim said, and when Charlie Daws swung down and Rim had mounted, he added, "I've got three thousand dollars in my saddlebags yonder." He pointed at his dead horse down the trail. "Some of you boys watch it. One of you stay with Tyler. I'm going to look for Bert Stallart."

CHAPTER SEVENTEEN

Eric Ward, standing in the yard at Anchor, hat in hand, gave the dark-haired woman a sad smile. Three older men, gray hair thickly tangled below hat brims, watched them from the bench in front of the bunkhouse.

"So you see, Mrs. Stallart," Ward said in his quiet, best country-gentleman manner, "I just want you to understand I have no control over Meade Jellick."

"But you hired him after he was fired from Anchor," Marcy Stallart said.

"I needed a horse breaker—" Ward spread his hands. "It's the same as if a man tried to make a pet out of a lion cub he found in the hills. All would go well until one day the growing cub tasted blood. That's how it is with Jellick. He was reasonably docile until the day he went berserk and killed your brother."

He saw her wince and swing her gaze toward the starkly erect headboards in the Anchor Bar burial ground on the knoll.

"I'm sorry about your brother," Ward said. "I'll see that Jellick pays for that among other things."

She brought her stricken gaze back to his face. "I don't understand you, Mr. Ward. You are my husband's enemy. You spread vile stories about me and—" Ward noticed the slight break in her voice—"my husband's partner."

"Believe me, I am truthful when I say that was Jellick's doing. Not mine."

"Was it also Jellick's doing—Jellick's alone—when two hundred head of Anchor cows were taken the day my brother was killed?"

"Mrs. Stallart, your husband and I were engaged in a business enterprise in Kansas. The cows you speak of were part payment on an old debt."

Her dark eyes studied him closely. "Why is it I can never get my husband to talk about Kansas?"

"This is something I can't explain."

"Was this business of yours so—so—" She waved a strong hand, groping for the word. "Something to be ashamed of?"

Ward deliberated a moment, then said, "Many things happened during the war that men would rather forget."

"I see."

He felt a little uncomfortable under her steady gaze. He knew she was not only handsome but possessed of brains as well. He had come here today with a twofold purpose in mind. To prepare her as much as he could for the death of her husband, that was inevitable. And to let her know that when she was widowed he, Eric Ward, was her friend and was to be trusted.

He wanted to get away from the grim slant their conversation had taken, and told her of the time before the war when he had been extended the hospitality of a plantation house during a storm. "Since that time I have had a fondness for that type of person. I know that you once came from such a home. You are extremely fortunate."

"Am I?"

The sharpness of her tone caused a small furrow to ridge his forehead. "I don't blame you for being bitter. It was a grand way of life. And, alas, it is gone forever."

"I daresay most of us will survive without it."

He felt that somehow he had offended her and his mind groped for the reason.

"It may have appeared to be a grand way of life, as you put it," she went on, "but it was a way of life dependent upon the enslavement of human beings."

He pursed his lips, nimbly swinging into the wake of her pronouncement: "I was an Abolitionist."

But even this didn't bring any lessening of her watchfulness. "Thank you for offering your friendship," she said coolly. "I'll tell my husband when he comes home."

He felt a surge of rage at her insolence. Didn't she realize that her husband was never coming home? That after smashing a whisky bottle against Meade Jellick's head, her husband was doomed? That Jellick would hunt down Bert Stallart, and there wasn't a human on this earth who could prevent the killing. The palms of his hands itched to grab her and push her into the house and make her realize that Eric Ward was the only man in this world she could have? Not Bert Stallart, not Rim Bolden. No one else—

She stood stiffly, hands clenched at her sides. And he had the eerie feeling that she almost sensed his thoughts. He said, "Remember, I am always at your service."

She said nothing, but just looked at him in that way of hers. She went into the house and closed the door.

Flushing, he strode to his horse. He jammed his hat on his head. What would she say if she knew at this very minute her husband lay dead, and probably also dead was Rim Bolden. For this day Jellick had planned to make a full sweep of his vengeance. Ward shivered a little when he thought of the raging Jellick who regained consciousness on the floor of the saloon in LaVentana. And Ward was considerably relieved to learn that Jellick didn't know who had struck him down that second time with the barrel of a gun. Not that Ward considered himself afraid of Jellick. But he knew if the man realized who had struck him that second time there would be a shooting. Ward didn't want to kill Jellick. And this he would be forced to do if Jellick came after him. He wanted Jellick to stay alive a little while longer. For the time being he was useful.

Turning in the saddle he looked around at the house and saw Mrs. Stallart watching him from one of the windows. She didn't know it yet, he thought, but that house, the other buildings, everything here would soon change ownership. "And that includes you, Marcy Stallart," he whispered to the still face in the window. He touched the brim of his hat with a long forefinger, and rode across the yard.

He stared at the three silent old men sitting stiffly in front of the bunkhouse. He nodded at them, and only one responded with, "Howdy, Mr. Ward." The other two glared at the speaker and the man shrugged and looked away.

Ward made a mental note to remember the man who had spoken. That man would be retained when Anchor Bar changed hands. The other two would be fired.

Ward had barely cleared the yard when the sudden appearance of a rider startled him. He had scouted this Anchor headquarters for half an hour before riding down to talk with Marcy Stallart, whom he had seen sunning herself beside the house. He was sure the Anchor crew was across the mountains at roundup camp. No one about the place but the three pensioners occupying the bench in front of the bunkhouse.

But now from the corner of his eye he saw this rider mottled by shadow in the trees. He reached for his gun, but a familiar voice said, "It's me, Ward. Pete Prentiss. I heard you were comin' this way. I been waitin' for you."

It was one of his own men, a ruddy-faced man with a worn patch over one eye. Despite this apparent handicap, the Prentiss vision was good enough to enable him to show a decided talent with a gun. Ward had sent clear down to Paso for him.

"What is it, Pete?" Ward demanded.

"Sid went lookin' for you in town, but I come over here. I remembered you sayin' this morning—"

"All right, all right," Ward said impatiently. "Has there been more trouble?" And he thought hopefully that it might be news that Stallart and Bolden were dead. And if this were the case Ward would ride back to the house and deliver the news in person and watch Marcy Stallart's face. She'd damn soon get over her imperious manner. It was galling, Ward thought, not to have made a better impression on her. He considered himself genteel and had thought she would soon realize that he was one of her kind.

But this pleasant contemplation was destroyed by Pete Prentiss who was falling all over his words in trying to impart some information. It was something about this girl being driven out from town by somebody from the livery stable, trunk and all. She had arrived in town and heard that the only T man in town was Tut Tyler. And she had got hold of Tyler and asked him to take a message out to T ranch. But this morning she had seen Tyler drunk and realized he hadn't delivered her message at all. So—

"Who did you say it was?" Ward demanded as he finally realized what Prentiss was talking about.

"Your sister."

Ward's mouth slowly opened. What a time to pick for a visit. He didn't want her here until this bloody business was ended. He would take her immediately back to town where she would stay until he decided it was time for her to console the Widow Stallart—

CHAPTER EIGHTEEN

Rim rode down through shin oak, his horse sliding on shale. At last he came to a trail of blood and followed it to his former partner. Stallart lay against a rock, his eyes open, gripping the revolver that lay on the ground at his side. At first Rim thought he was dead.

Rim dismounted and came closer, seeing the hole in Stallart's thigh. He saw another hole in the front of his shirt. But there was not much bleeding from this wound as there was with the one Tut Tyler had suffered.

He was five feet from Stallart when the man suddenly lifted the revolver. "Jellick!" Stallart cried in a voice hoarse from shock. "I should've killed you back in Kansas when I had the chance—"

Rim threw himself flat as the gun crashed. He sensed rather than felt the bullet go through the crown of his hat. Then he was on Stallart, twisting the gun free. But the move was unnecessary. The effort of shouting, of firing the gun seemed to have sapped the last of Stallart's strength. He was out cold.

Then other Anchor men were coming up, among them Ed Rule. "Did you and Bert have it out, Rim?" the cook asked, after looking around.

Rim shook his head. He felt a trembling in his legs as he told how he had come unexpectedly upon Jellick and the other two. He was lucky to be alive. But how much luck was a man entitled to in one lifetime.

The cook shook his gray head. "You got a hole in your hat, Rim. Somebody come almighty near to spillin' your brains."

Rim swallowed. His throat was tight and dry. "Let's carry Stallart down to the road. Some of you get back to camp and bring up a wagon. Tyler's up there," Rim pointed, "bad hit. Maybe he'll last till town, but I doubt it."

"One thing for sure," Ed Rule said, as the men hurried to carry out Rim's orders. "If it hadn't been for you buyin' into this game Stallart would be dead for sure."

"Yeah."

"Well, it ain't your fight no longer, Rim."

Rim looked at the cook. "And how about you? Is it your fight?"

"Reckon," the cook said without looking up. "I felt like cussin' Bert out a few minutes back. But when it's a war like this—Well, a man draws pay from an outfit he sticks with it till the thing is settled."

Rim looked around at the other men, those in the saddle, those now starting to carry Stallart down to the road to meet the wagon. "That's the way it is with all of us," Rim said. "We'll stick till the thing is settled."

Rim was surprised to hear Stallart's voice, clouded with pain, and realized the rancher had regained consciousness and evidently had heard everything that had been said.

"You don't have to stick, Rim," Stallart said. "You don't owe me nothin'."

Rim walked beside the improvised stretcher, each of four men holding a corner of a blanket one of them had unlashed from the back of a saddle.

Rim saw that Stallart's eyes reflected the shock that gripped his big body. "Maybe I owe myself something, Bert," Rim said. "A man quits a fight and he'll be quitting for the rest of his life."

"I—I heard what you said about Jellick. You saved my hide. Thanks, but maybe my hide ain't worth savin'."

"You better not talk, Bert. It's a long way to Doc Snider's place."

They reached the road and put Stallart in the shade to await the wagon from camp.

"Send the boys away, Rim," Stallart said with painful slowness. "I want to talk to you—alone."

Rim didn't have to order this done for Ed Rule jerked his head at the men and they went on down the road some twenty yards to stand in a close-knit group, talking in low tones. Overhead the sky had darkened; clouds, big and black, tore themselves against the higher peaks.

Rim dropped to one knee. "How's it going, Bert?"

"Not bad, all things considered."

"The pain will come when the shock wears off. You'd better be prepared for it."

"Don't worry. This ain't the first time I been shot. I got a favor to ask, Rim."

"Go ahead. Ask it. Things have changed since this shooting. I'm still your partner. No papers were signed."

"Like I said, you don't owe me nothin'."

"Maybe, maybe not. But I owe something to Marcy."

For an instant there was a steel-bright glitter in Stallart's eyes. Then it was gone.

"I admire her. I respect her," Rim went on. "If I don't take hold now she'll have nothing. She doesn't deserve that, Bert."

"You had your chance," Stallart said. "Why didn't you let Jellick finish me? Then you and Marcy—"

"She still loves you, Bert. Though God only knows why after the way you've treated her."

"The favor I asked, Rim. Tie me to a saddle. Tie a gun to my hand. Take me to Jellick."

"You couldn't set a saddle straight, no matter how much tying a man did."

"I just want to live long enough to kill him."

"We had a lot of chances for that, Bert," Rim said. "After he killed Simpson. Especially after he killed Willie and the others."

"If I die then you and Marcy—"

"That's enough, Bert."

"A thing happens to a man once in his life. Then it's easier to believe if you think it happens again."

Moisture lay in deep trenches on Stallart's weathered forehead, sparkled at the ends of his mustache. In the distance was the clatter of an approaching wagon.

"Let's finish it, Bert," Rim said. "What happened between you and Jellick back in Kansas?"

The cords in Stallart's throat tightened as he swallowed. "It ain't an easy thing to tell."

"Your damn foolishness is going to ruin the life of a fine woman. Think of her if not of yourself."

"Any way it turns out, Rim," Stallart said weakly, "me and Marcy are done."

"Let her decide that."

Stallart turned his head, looking toward the brushy slope. "How you reckon she'll feel when she knows I killed my own brother. Shot him dead eight years back."

"Your brother Paul. Ellamae's father."

"It's why I wanted to do something for the gal. But she—she's just like Paul was. Layin' with a man and gettin' herself a bastard."

"I imagine she's paid for that in more ways than one."

"Ellamae's ma died when the gal was just a kid. Paul left Ellamae with a woman in Joplin to raise. So far as I know Ellamae figured this Aunt Rose was her real kin. After Paul died I paid the woman for Ellamae's keep. But last year this woman died and Ellamae kept writing me and wanting to come out. But I held off because seein' her would remind me of what I done to her pa. But then she wrote that she *had* to come—"

"And Jellick knows you killed your brother?"

"Yeah. I was married to a woman Jellick used to run around with. I was doin' right well. But it was when the war come along and there was trouble in Kansas and I was gone a lot. Paul come to visit me. I—I come home one night—They was foolin' together. I beat Paul up and he got a gun and we fought over it. The gun went off."

"And your wife?"

"She—she run away. She told Jellick about it. Jellick owned a saloon then." Stallart clenched his hands. "She died of cholera that same year."

Rim wiped off the beading of perspiration from Stallart's forehead with a bandanna. "And you came here and tried to build a new life."

"Everybody back in Kansas liked Paul. He was that kind of a fella. Bought drinks, always had a good story to tell. They hated me for killin' him. Never no mind that he broke up my home. He was my *brother*." Stallart groaned and there was a flash of pain in his eyes. "The sheriff come for me and they had a trial and they was goin' to hang me at sunrise. I busted outa jail—"

"Jellick trailed you here?"

"He come through LaVentana last year with a freight outfit. I didn't figure he seen me. But then he comes back and tells me he wants a job and I hire him on as hoss breaker. And it was a little before that when Eric Ward starts his outfit and tries to tell me he knows all about what happened in Kansas. I got scared as hell. Nobody wants to hang."

"When Jellick started spreading his poison about Marcy and me—Well, you should have considered the source."

"One woman goes bad on you and you'll believe most anything."

"But believing Jellick." Rim shook his head. "Bert, you should have told me this before."

"I'm a dead man, Rim. All Jellick and Ward have to do is get word to Kansas. But I'd rather all my blood leaked out on the ground right here than go back to Kansas and die at the end of a rope."

"So Ward and Jellick just figured to help themselves to Anchor Bar cows whenever they felt like it."

"They said they'd settle for a thousand head. Two hundred at a time. They took the first bunch and I give 'em a bill-of-sale and Willie went after 'em—"

"They'd never stop at a thousand head. They'd keep on until they drained Anchor of everything on four feet."

"Yeah." Stallart looked up at him, and there was a grayness now about the mouth. "It's why I wanted a good foreman, a good partner, Rim. I had to trail cows to Kansas. But I couldn't go myself. I had to have somebody I could trust."

"Sure, Bert." Rim got to his feet. "Here comes the wagon."

When Stallart was placed on a pile of blankets the wagon moved on up the road, the team straining against their harness.

"What you aim to do, Rim?" Ed Rule said.

"I aim," Rim said, "to take a double rope and hang Meade Jellick. I aim to hang Eric Ward beside him."

CHAPTER NINETEEN

April looked around the small, poorly-furnished room. This wasn't her brother's place. It couldn't be. There were cracks in the wall and she could see daylight; and a small scurrying animal drifted in, flashed across the room and disappeared into another crack. She shuddered and clenched her fists. Through the dirty window that was broken and made tight by a rag stuffed into the opening, she could see two men in the yard. They were tough-looking and not at all as she pictured Eric's crew to be.

It seemed that she waited hours before hearing the sound of horses. She went to the door and looked out and saw Eric and a one-eyed man come up the steep road on lathered horses.

Eric saw her step from the house. He dismounted and came across the yard. He didn't seem particularly glad to see her and she felt a moment of disillusionment. And worse, she felt unwanted.

"This is rather a surprise," Eric said coldly. He didn't kiss her cheek or shake her hand or embrace her. He just took her by the arm and led her back into the house and closed the door. "Just what in the world possessed you to make the trip out here?"

"You wrote that you wanted me. I just thought—"

"But I wanted you later." As he paced the uneven floor she saw dust puff up from the loose boards under his feet. He turned, eying her. "I think you're presumptuous to take this on yourself. This trip, and unchaperoned—"

"You told me you wanted me to learn self-reliance," she said. "You paid for my education at the Holendale Academy. They specialize in teaching young ladies self—"

"I know, I know." He put a hand to his face and stared darkly out the window. "How long have you been in town?"

She told him and he gave a great sigh of exasperation. "Why in the world didn't you go to the sheriff?" he demanded. "Or some other responsible person and have them send someone to let me know?"

"This man who said his name was Tyler. He was in the hotel lobby and I heard him say he worked for you. I asked him to take a message to you." The shoulders under the green traveling dress shrugged. "But when you didn't come I asked someone and they said this Tut Tyler had been drunk and never left town. So I hired a buggy and came myself with a man from the livery stable."

"Well, you used poor judgment in trusting Tyler."

"I'd like to know why," she said, her gray eyes studying the handsome face—a little drawn now—of this man who was her only living relative. That he had been good to her she couldn't deny. When their father died he sent her to the academy and provided her with enough money so she could live in the style demanded by a student in the school. She tried to explain to him now that she didn't want the useless life of a lady. She wanted to live in stimulating country such as this. Couldn't he understand that?

No, he couldn't understand it at all. "You'll have to return to town," Eric Ward said shortly.

She went to him, her skirts dragging on the dusty floor. "Eric, are you in some kind of trouble?"

"No. I'm just put out that you'd take it upon yourself to make this trip without advising me beforehand."

"Eric, I have no one in the world but you. I thought we should be together. Why wait until you brought a herd to Kansas? Why not now? Life is so short. We both know that."

"Just what in the world do you think you can do here?" His voice was rough.

A flush of anger touched her cheeks. "I thought I could cook for you. Keep house. But if you don't want me—"

"Keep house in a place like this?" he demanded.

"I'll admit it isn't exactly as you pictured it."

"No, I suppose not," he said, lowering his voice. "This is only temporary headquarters. I—I'm negotiating for another ranch. I didn't want you to come until I had need for you."

"And just when would you need me?" she said thinly.

"I intend courting a widow. When the time is right I want you to meet her, to become friends. She is a lady and so are you. I hope. I've spent enough on your education to make you one."

"Thank you," she said stiffly. "I thought you sent me to the academy for other reasons. I didn't know I was supposed to act as an intermediary in your romances—"

"That's enough. You don't know anything about it, so don't try and guess. The thing to do now is get you back to town."

"Why not introduce me to this widow now?"

"Because she isn't a widow yet—"

"I thought so." She stood with hands clasped under her breasts, watching this man she hardly knew.

"Just what in hell did you mean by that?"

"No need to curse," she said. "You're going to kill this woman's husband, aren't you?"

"No. And what gave you that idea?"

"I heard many stories about you, Eric. Why you left St. Louis suddenly—"

"You believe gossip about your brother?" he said, and tried to smile.

"They say you cheated at cards. That you're a gunman."

"You were willing enough to take that sort of money for your education," he reminded.

"I didn't know about it then. Not until I was through at the academy."

"Any man who wins at cards is called a cheat by those who lose," he said, obviously fighting to control his voice. "As for being a gunman—" He shrugged. "I'm fortunate enough to possess a certain talent of sorts. Otherwise, I would be dead."

"And I also heard gossip in LaVentana. When I would sit in the hotel lobby. People didn't know who I was and I would hear them talk. They like you, Eric. And you have charm, I know that. I've seen you use it. But they're worried."

"Worried because a man named Bert Stallart owes me money and—"

"Is it Mrs. Stallart who is to be the widow you will court?"

"If you must know, yes."

"They say she is quite handsome. They worry because of a possible range war between your ranch and the Stallart's."

"Nonsense. It's Stallart's doings. His and that thief foreman of his, Rim Bolden."

"Let me tell you about Rim Bolden," she said.

"You know him?" Eric Ward asked his sister in surprise.

She told of witnessing the historic fight on her way to LaVentana. "He whipped this giant of a man."

"And he'll die for it. Jellick will kill him. And as long as we're on the subject, Jellick will also kill Stallart. I'll have nothing to do with it. As a matter of fact," he added quietly, "Stallart is probably already dead."

"Then this Meade Jellick does work for you," April said. "It's one thing I didn't believe. That my brother would hire a man like that."

"One thing you've got to realize, April. This isn't St. Louis. This is tough country. You fight fire with fire. Stallart has Rim Bolden. I have Jellick. It adds up to the same thing, no matter how Bolden may have impressed you."

"He's a gentleman. I remember he reacted strangely when I said you were my brother."

"No wonder," he said, watching her closely. "He's my enemy."

"Eric, just what sort of a game are you playing here?"

"A game that can make us both rich, April. You might as well realize one fact. Since the war things have changed. There are no longer any decent values in life. A man makes his own way with his wits."

"And with his gun."

"If you want to put it that way, yes. It's defend yourself or be buried. As simple as that."

"I don't think the world has changed so much since the war. I intend to raise my children in this world—"

"You'll be married in time," he said abruptly, "to someone I select."

"So that's the reason for your great care to have me educated at the academy. You want to use me as a pawn."

"I want you to marry well. If your marriage benefits us both in a political way, for instance, what is the harm of that?"

"I appreciate what you've done for me, Eric, but—"

"Then show your gratitude by going back to town and staying there until this is over. Better yet, I'll send you down to Mesilla."

"So I'll be comfortably out of the way when you start this bloody business against your neighbor Stallart." She hesitated, adding, "And his foreman."

He gave her a sharp, speculative look. "Don't tell me you've fallen for this Rim Bolden."

She looked away. "I didn't say I had. I only know this that if I had to choose impartially between your men and Stallart's, I'd take the latter."

"I see the academy gave you a special course in insolence."

"The academy taught me to think for myself. To stand up for myself."

"You'll do what I tell you, and no nonsense."

"I'm not a chattel, Eric. Just because we're related is no reason for you to assume as much."

She got no chance to pursue the subject further because at that moment she saw Meade Jellick come into the yard on a big horse with an ugly wound across a foreleg. Even though the animal was hurt she could see that Jellick had used the spurs unmercifully. Her half-brother went out to meet him, looking worried all of a sudden. April came to stand in the doorway, trying to overhear.

They talked earnestly and once she caught the name of Rim Bolden. She noted with satisfaction that Jellick still bore the marks of his fight with Bolden. There were bruises on his face, his eyes were still swollen. Around his head was a dirty, bloodied bandage.

Eric Ward said loudly, "Damn it, Meade, why did you have to let your private hatred of Stallart nearly ruin things? I told you we had him if we just kept our wits. You got mixed up with his niece and—"

"Stallart took a woman away from me once. I ain't forgot."

"Forget Kansas."

"He also busted a bottle over my head." Jellick paused, then added, "I'll also get the other fella that hit me, Eric, sure as hell I will."

"Well, it wasn't me."

"Maybe not." Then Jellick, catching sight of April in the doorway whispered something to Ward.

Ward came toward the house and Jellick hurried down to the corral for a fresh horse.

"Maybe you'll be happy to learn," Ward said when he took her back inside, "that your friend Rim Bolden and Stallart jumped some of my boys. Bolden killed two of them. Stallart is dead. But Bolden got away."

"I don't believe you," she said, and felt the blood leave her face.

"I don't expect you to. You've turned against your own kin. Remember the man you gave the message to? Tut Tyler? He's one of them. Bolden's hated him ever since Tyler couldn't stomach his high-handed ways and came to work for me. Bolden saw his chance to kill him and he did."

She stood stiffly, not knowing what she could say.

Eric said, "Just so you'll see that I'm not quite the gunman you seem to think I am, we're bringing the sheriff into this. Letting him settle it. You're coming to town with us."

"I—"

"Can you ride a horse?"

"A little. Sidesaddle."

"We don't have a sidesaddle. Nor a wagon. You'll have to ride the best way you can. We'll move slowly."

"But this dress—I can't straddle a horse like a man."

"My dear April, if you had waited to come out when I sent for you, all these civilized comforts, so to speak, would have been provided. But under the circumstances, you'll just have to make the best of it."

Eric helped her into the saddle of a small gray horse and she flushed when her skirts climbed halfway up her legs, exposing her limbs. She saw Eric glaring at the men who glanced at her. The men rode out ahead.

Meade Jellick said, "Ma'am, I busted that hoss myself. He'll be gentle."

She did not answer.

Eric, riding at her side, kept looking back toward the timbered ridges. At last he said, "We'll have to hurry it up."

She looked back and saw what had concerned him—a distant spiral of dust that seemed to be moving toward the ranch headquarters they had just left.

They increased their pace and she had a hard time staying aboard. Eric was sweating, looking worried. But she couldn't think of much else, only retaining her seat on this "gentle" horse. It seemed to move with an ungainly stride, not like the sleek purebreds she'd ridden sidesaddle at the academy. She was forced to cling to the saddle horn with both hands and once she dropped the reins and they dangled about the gray's forelegs. He shied and she nearly fell. Eric, cutting in close, brought the horse under control.

Meade Jellick said, "Eric, my head is hurtin' something fierce. I got to see the doc when I get to town. I can't stand this pounding. I got to slow up."

"Keep moving," Eric snapped, and glanced toward the mountains again.

Jellick said, "You boys go on ahead. Me an' your sister will take it easy. If she don't she's goin' to fall outa that saddle and get trampled."

"Yes, maybe you're right. Keep out of sight as much as possible, Meade. If Anchor comes—Well, we're only five miles from town. I don't think they'll bother you."

April felt a slow chilling fear begin to build in her. "Eric, I want to go with you."

"I want the sheriff to have us sworn in as deputies by the time Anchor gets to town," Eric said. "They'll be sure to trail us there from the ranch."

"But Eric—"

"You can't keep up with us." She saw her half-brother give Meade Jellick a sharp glance. "I'm trusting you, Meade. You know what I mean."

"I got me a sickness in the head," Jellick said. "Don't worry none."

And he did look ill. He kept closing his swollen eyes. She thought maybe the wound under the bandage had started to bleed again, but she couldn't be sure.

"Eric, leave me your revolver," she said. "I'll feel better if you do."

Eric Ward licked his lips, hesitated, then drew an extra revolver from his saddlebags. He moved close, dropped the weapon in the gray's saddlebags. "You'll be in town before you know it." Then he and the other three men spurred on ahead.

For a half mile she and Meade Jellick rode at a walk without speaking. Then she saw a stone rolling in front of her horse. She never did know whether Jellick had thrown it or whether it had come down from a brushy bank to the right of the road. Her horse started to pitch and she felt a surging panic, but Jellick came in close. He caught the bridle and jerked the horse around with his terrible strength, quieting it. And she saw to her horror that with the other hand he had drawn from her saddlebags the revolver Eric had given her. Jellick threw the weapon far into the trees that bordered the north side of the road.

"Tut Tyler was drunk out back of the Jewel and he looked through the window and seen your brother hit me over the head with a gun," Jellick said. "I felt like killin' Eric. I will. But first I'll give him something to sweat about. Get down off that hoss!"

CHAPTER TWENTY

Rim decided against trying to take Bert Stallart all the way to LaVentana in the wagon. It would be better to leave him at Anchor. And besides, this was what Stallart wanted. He was against going to town. Rim sent a rider on ahead to alert Doc Snider. There was a possibility, however slim, that the doctor might be able to reach headquarters within the hour of the wagon's arrival.

In order to make sure Jellick didn't try to finish his murderous day, Rim ordered some of his men to accompany the wagon. He then sent five riders to headquarters to guard the ranch buildings and Marcy Stallart, for there was no telling what Jellick and Ward might try next. Then with ten men he rode for Ward's T ranch. Forgotten was roundup. Let the herd they had started to build drift back into the hills. Nothing mattered now but settling with the enemy. There was no other way. If Jellick and Ward won this private war then Anchor was finished.

They picked up Jellick's trail some five miles from the scene of the shooting. From the sign Rim could tell that the horse was limping badly. He couldn't be too far ahead of them.

Now that the heat of the sudden fight in the hills, his killing of two men, the confession of Stallart, had faded a little, Rim wondered just how he felt about his partner. Or was it ex-partner? He had voiced some platitudes back there, about loyalty to one's outfit, one's partner. No matter what a trying few weeks it had been with this partner. How much better it would have been if Stallart had disclosed the reasons for Jellick and Ward acting as they had. A lot of lives would have been saved. No matter how this turned out he would always blame Stallart for letting Jellick not only push him into a corner, but fill his head with vicious gossip.

How much better if Bert Stallart, following the bitter experience with his first wife, had married a homely woman. One that a man would find it hard to suspect of anything at all. It was Stallart's bad luck that he had married a woman of Marcy's good looks. And it went without saying that it was also Marcy's bad luck—

After a cautious approach to Ward's headquarters they found the place deserted. Then they saw the sign; six riders had headed east not too long ago.

"We'll use those ropes yet, boys," Rim said. "They can't be far ahead of us."

They followed the trail that led toward LaVentana. One thing puzzled Rim as he studied the tracks left by the six horses. The cavalcade was moving slowly. Apparently in no hurry. He felt uneasy. Was Ward setting up an ambush? Hoping they'd follow this main trail and leave themselves open for an attack on their flanks.

Then in the distance he saw two saddle horses tied off in the trees. He dismounted, told the men to wait for him and went on afoot. He cut through some junipers bordering the road, trying to keep downwind from the two tied horses. Then something vividly green caught his eye. He paused, feeling his heart lurch. He hurried forward. The green was a length of green cloth, a woman's dress, as he had feared. It was torn, trampled into the dust. He remembered such a dress worn by April Ward the day of his fight with Jellick.

Cocked gun in his sweating hand, he moved forward. And the two saddle horses caught his scent and neighed.

Above this warning sound he heard a girl's fierce sobs. And Jellick saying, "You might as well make up your mind to it—"

"The horses!" the girl cried. "Somebody's here! Help!"

And then Rim was through a waist-high screen of brush. "Easy, Jellick," he warned.

Meade Jellick, head lifted now to peer in the direction of the whinnying horses tied off in the trees, whirled. When he saw the gun pointed at his belly, he pushed his hands wide from his big body.

April was moving crab-wise across the dusty ground. Dust stained a long undergarment that had narrow green ribbons at neckline and hem. Her gray eyes were wide with terror, as her gaze swung from Rim to Jellick. She got up, crouched like some animal ready to flee.

"See if there's enough left of that dress to cover you," Rim said, without taking his eyes from Jellick. Then he raised his voice, shouting, "Come on, boys! I've got Jellick!"

By the time they rode up April had slipped into the dress, holding the torn length about her. The Anchor men surrounded Jellick, disarmed him, tied his hands behind his back.

Jellick spoke for the first time. "Bolden, you're too yellow to go for me man to man with a gun."

"Since when do you call yourself a man?"

The Anchor crew stood around uncomfortably, all too aware of what had been about to take place here had it not been for Rim's interference. The girl stood watching them. There was a streak of dust on her hair, a smudge on one cheek. She looked frightened.

"You ride with us," Rim told her. "You'll be safe with Mrs. Stallart."

"My—my brother has gone to LaVentana—"

"You come with us," Rim said, and tried to find some reason for a gentle girl like this having Eric Ward for a brother. A man who would think so little of her that he'd give Meade Jellick an opportunity to get her alone.

"What'll we do with him, Rim?" Ed Rule said.

"I think Bert Stallart ought to see this."

When they were riding toward Anchor, Rim saw to it that April brought up the rear so the men couldn't stare at her. She was hardly dressed for sitting a saddle. And she had to keep one hand holding the dress together.

"What are you going to do with him?" she asked in a small frightened voice.

"Something I should have done a long time ago," Rim answered.

"My brother has gone for the sheriff. Jellick can be turned over to him."

Rim made no reply, trying to keep his mind off the anger that was churning in him. But at last he could no longer restrain himself. "Just how did you happen to be alone with Jellick?"

She told him.

Rim shook his head slowly from side to side. "And you say Ward is your brother."

"Half-brother."

"He acts as if you were a complete stranger."

"Ward has problems. I suppose he just didn't think." When he looked back at her he saw that her head was bowed. He saw a tear fall against the horn of the saddle. "Thank you for what you did, Mr. Bolden."

They said nothing more until they at last reached Anchor headquarters. He saw the wagon in the yard, saw the rest of his men. Now as he had many times in the past, he wished he had a seasoned, tough, gunfighting crew. But you couldn't expect a bonus like that when you hired men for cowman's pay.

"I see you got Jellick," one of the men said with satisfaction.

"Yep, we got him."

"How soon you figure to swing him?"

"Right away. How's Stallart?"

"Tolerable. We carried him into the house. Doc Snider oughta be comin' directly."

Rim rode up to where April waited by the house. He dismounted, helped her from the saddle. She had to grip the dress with both hands to keep it from falling apart. He hurried her into the house. Marcy, standing in the center of the big kitchen, wearing a gray dress, looked startled.

"Will you help her, Marcy?" Rim said. "She's had a bad experience. Miss Ward, this is Marcy Stallart."

"How do you do," April said in a shaking voice.

Marcy said, "Come upstairs, my dear. I think I have a dress that will fit you."

Marcy directed the fat Mexican cook to take April to an upstairs bedroom. "I'll be up in a minute."

And when April and the Mexican woman had gone, Rim said, "Marcy, I want you to take her to a back bedroom. I want you to stay there with her."

She gave him a questioning glance, then through the kitchen window she saw Meade Jellick throwing his giant's shadow against the bunkhouse wall. He was surrounded by armed Anchor men.

"I don't want either of you women to see it," Rim said. "Understand?" He touched her arm. "How's Bert."

"He'll recover. Providing he has the will to recover." She made a small gesture. "He babbled something about how badly he treated me and how sorry he is. About a killing back in Kansas."

"He'll try and make it up to you, Marcy. Give him a chance."

In Stallart's bedroom Rim said, "We've got Jellick." And he caught hold of the foot of the bed where Stallart lay and hauled and pushed it against the window that overlooked the yard. "He's cost you so much, Bert," Rim said. "I feel it's your privilege to see this."

"Open the window, Rim," Stallart said feebly. He was in his underwear and Marcy had bandaged his chest. There was another bulky bandage on his thigh. He seemed in better shape than Rim had expected.

Rim got the window open and Stallart looked down into the yard. "How goes it, Jellick?" he called.

Jellick peered up at the window, no expression on his bruised face.

"I want to get on with this, Bert," Rim said.

"What about Ward?"

Rim looked bitter as he thought of the red-haired girl in the other bedroom. "When this job is done, then I'll take care of him. I'm against this sort of thing usually. But what can you do when we have a sheriff who is more interested in clay heads than in doing his job?"

"Use a stout rope on him, Rim."

In the yard Rim studied the beams that jutted from the bunkhouse wall. "Think one of them will hold him, Ed?" he asked the cook.

"Worth a try," Ed Rule said, and spat so that the spittle touched a toe of Jellick's boots. Jellick turned red. "If it was me," the old cook went on, "I'd do like the 'Paches when one of their women gets raped. Cook his feet till he begs you to kill him."

"We're not savages," Rim said.

"You claim there's anything civilized about what he was goin' to do to that poor gal?"

Rim had some of the men scout the barn for a heavy rope. In a few moments they came out with one and Rim ordered a noose tied at one end. They got a barrel and one of the men climbed to the bunkhouse roof and tied the end of the rope to one of the beams.

"A little higher," Rim instructed. "We want to be sure his feet are off the ground. That rope may stretch."

The man re-tied it and climbed down. They got a short length of rope and tied Jellick's ankles. The man tried to kick, but four of them got him steadied until the knot was tied.

A grayness touched Jellick's face as if he realized for the first time that this was no bluff. They intended going through with it.

"Listen, Bolden," Jellick began, and Rim noted with satisfaction that his voice was shaking.

"You're hanging for many reasons," Rim interrupted. "Take a look at the headboards in the graveyard yonder. Count the reasons."

Jellick began to scream and Rim gave an anxious glance toward the house. "Gag him," he ordered, and a dirty bandanna was forced between Jellick's teeth and tied behind his head.

It took five men to boost the struggling Jellick up on the barrel; two men on horseback, helping to haul him up. One of the riders got the rope around Jellick's neck.

Rim walked up to the barrel, saw that it was steady. Jellick stood very still, for it would be easy to tip the barrel if he shifted his weight. He stared down, and perspiration dripped from his face into the dust beside the barrel. His eyes were alive with screaming, but because of the gag no sound came from him.

"I'd ask if you have any last words, Jellick," Rim said. "But under the circumstances you couldn't talk even if you wanted to."

Rim drew back his right foot to kick the barrel out from under Jellick.

Then he heard a commotion at the kitchen door, and April screaming, "Stop! Stop!"

Rim turned, seeing her in the doorway. Marcy was slightly behind her, trying to pull the girl back into the house. With a violent twisting of her shoulders, April got away from the older woman and rushed across the yard. The men stood aside, looking as uncomfortable as some of them had earlier when Rim had found her with Jellick. She wore one of Marcy's brown dresses that was too snug at bosom and hips.

"Don't do this," she said to Rim, her voice shaking. "There is the law—"

"I'm sorry," Rim said. "Will you go back into the house, or will I have to carry you in?"

She stood up to him, her face flushed, fists clenched at her sides. "Just because of what he—he tried to do to me." Color deepened even more on her face, but she did not lower her eyes. "Please, don't make me think of you as a butcher. Please—The law can take care of him."

He waved a brown hand toward the graveyard on the knoll beyond the bunkhouse. "When this is over, go up and look at the headboards there. The new ones are a result of Jellick's murderous gun. Now get back in the house!"

For an answer she whirled to a man standing nearby, deftly drew a knife from his belt. With the blade flashing in the sunlight she stepped quickly behind Jellick. She tried to reach the thongs that bound his wrists. "Better that he be turned loose," she said in a voice strangled with hysteria, "than bring blood down on your own head!"

With an oath Rim grabbed her. He swung her up in his arms, knocking the knife from her hand. It lay glittering in the dust.

"Rim, Rim!" she sobbed. "Don't make me hate you. Don't make me!"

He started for the house with her and she kicked and squirmed and screamed.

All the Anchor men in the yard were watching Rim and the girl and therefore did not see the riders who left their horses some distance away and crept up afoot.

But Rim saw them and at the same time heard Eric Ward's voice. "Put down my sister, Bolden. Get your hands up! Every last man of you!"

"Do what he says!" Sheriff Jared Dort cut in. "This is the law!"

CHAPTER TWENTY-ONE

There were some twenty-five men who had come up quietly through the trees that masked the southern entrance to Anchor headquarters. Rim saw some of his men lift their rifles and instantly he thought of the safety of this girl in his arms. The safety of Marcy Stallart, standing as if frozen by the kitchen door. In the distance came the sounds of a team, the whirring of wheels. Doc Snider, Rim thought.

Being careful to make no overt move, Rim set April on her feet. She brushed her hair away from her eyes, "Eric, thank God you've come."

She started toward her half-brother and he said, "I don't know how you got here, but get into the house! Stay there!"

"But, Eric—"

"Do what I tell you!"

Run saw the girl give her brother a puzzled look, then move to the house. She and Marcy went inside, leaving the door ajar.

Slowly Ward came toward Rim, holding a rifle. At his left was Sheriff Dort, looking grim, his pants splattered with dried clay. A badge on the front of Ward's shirt caught the sunlight. Pete Prentiss, his eye patch dusty, his good eye watching them, also wore a badge.

Rim said, "Dort, I see you've deputized Ward and Prentiss. To me it means the law here is several degrees lower than the underside of a snake."

"You Anchor men put down your guns," Sheriff Dort ordered. "Somebody cut Jellick loose."

Rim shook his head. "You have no right to interfere. In our eyes this is a legal execution."

"If Jellick slips off that barrel," Sheriff Dort warned, "I'll see you hang for murder."

"Murder? Evidently you don't know the meaning of the word." Rim's gaze was bitter. "After all the killing Jellick has done—at Ward's instigation."

"I've come with warrants, Bolden," the sheriff said and from his pocket drew two legal-looking documents. "One for you."

"And what's the charge?" Rim demanded, wondering if he could prolong this sufficiently to give himself time to consider a way out. At present there seemed none. Not unless he gave the word and they started to slaughter each other.

"You killed two of Ward's men," the sheriff said. "Tut Tyler and a man named Elson. That's what your warrant is for."

"They fired on me first."

"Ward says no. Anyhow, that's for a jury to decide." Dort looked around. "Where's Stallart? I'm arresting him for the murder of his brother back in Kansas. I'll personally escort him there."

Rim felt the slow beat of his pulse. He tried to listen for the sound of hoofs and wheels he had heard a minute or so ago. Only silence now. A man sneezed. There was the metallic click as a shell was levered into a rifle. The tension was thicker in the yard than Texas dust.

The Anchor men were watching him, waiting for some sign. He knew if he gave the word there would be carnage. Ward had the law on his side, no mistake about that. In the posse were townsmen. He recognized Allie Grindge of the Jewel Saloon, peering at him through his steel-rimmed spectacles. There was Harris from the Mountain Store and Perkins from the livery.

"It's best to let the sheriff do it his way, Rim," Allie Grindge said. "We got enough trouble around here as it is. You'll git a fair trial."

"As much chance of that as there'd be of one day voting Sherman mayor of Atlanta," he told the saloonman. "Get back to the Jewel, Allie, and take the rest of the boys with you."

"It's where I should be," Grindge said. "A lot of us are losing money being here. The outfits south of town have finished roundup. The town's full—"

"Hurry, Allie," Rim said from a corner of his mouth, "or you might lose four dollars worth of whisky business."

Grindge flushed. "Rim, you got no right—"

"Shut up, Allie," the sheriff said impatiently.

A shaggy head suddenly appeared in an upstairs window. A rifle barrel was shoved through the opening. Bert Stallart said in a voice that was little more than a harsh whisper, "Sheriff, you stand hitched or you'll be dead as my brother-in-law Willie."

Dort swung around, his face going slack as he saw Bert Stallart lying flat on a bed shoved against the open window. Stallart's face was without its usual coloring, and the mouth under the downsweeping mustache seemed taut with pain.

"Pick him off!" Eric Ward shouted, but the sheriff warned, "Hold it, Eric. Damn it, I'm the one he's got the rifle on. Not you. Stallart, now you listen here to me. I got a warrant—"

"You eat that goddam warrant," Stallart said. Rim, watching his partner tensely, saw the rifle barrel trembling in Stallart's grasp. Hold it, Rim urged silently. Just one more minute. He started edging toward Dort, eying the man's revolver, intending to knock it out of the man's hand.

But at that moment he saw Stallart stiffened and glance behind him. A shrill female voice said from the room, "Get on your feet, Uncle Bert. Get up and walk. Like you're going to do when you climb the gallows for killing my father!"

And Rim saw Ellamae framed in the window behind Bert Stallart. Saw the yellow hat with the feather in it, the bright yellow dress. The white-powdered face with its garish smear of lip paint. In her right hand she held a small ladies' revolver pointed at her uncle's back.

Stallart turned, made a grab for her, but the pain of his wounds must have been too much. He collapsed across the bed, and the rifle clattered down into the yard.

It had all taken just a few seconds, but it seemed like an age to Rim. As he saw the rifle slip from his partner's grasp he drew his gun, got in behind the sheriff. But Pete Prentiss fired, and the bullet touched the buckle of Rim's belt, denting it. The force of the blow knocked him down. As the bullet screamed in ricochet he heard Ed Rule grunt behind him. Dazed, Rim picked himself up, saw the ring of guns facing him. Saw Ed Rule sitting on the ground. The cook's right arm pumped a steady scarlet stream. A wisp of smoke drift from the muzzle of the one-eyed Pete Prentiss' gun. Prentiss shifted the weapon to cover Rim, drew back the hammer for another shot.

But Sheriff Dort managed to say shakily, "Hold it, Prentiss!" He came up, kicked Rim's gun aside.

It took Rim several moments to get his breath. He felt nausea grip him and he wanted to lie down in the dust and retch. Only the slight shifting of aim, and the bullet would have torn into his stomach.

He tried to anchor his feet into the ground but the world seemed to tilt under him. He saw everyone looking toward the house, and turned. Bert Stallart, hunched over, looking a hundred years old, limped out of the house. He was clad only in pants and socks. His upper body was covered by a thick bandage. The wound at his thigh had come open, staining the leg of his pants.

Behind him came Marcy and April, their hands lifted. Ellamae, still gripping her revolver, said, "Here's my dear uncle, Sheriff. Take him."

Stallart's bad leg went out from under him at that moment, and he pitched over into the yard. With a small cry Marcy sprang forward. She sank down, cradling her husband's head in her lap. She glared at Ellamae in the doorway. "You fool. You poor, poor fool."

"He killed my father!"

Not a man in the yard moved when Stallart managed to lift his head. "I did kill—your father," Stallart said haltingly. "It was—accident. Paul—he was no good—he ruined your mother's life—After you was born she didn't want to live—she just give up. Your pa the same as killed her—"

"I don't believe you!" Ellamae cried.

"It's—it's God's truth."

April, tears streaming down her face, cried, "Eric, do something! This is wrong. You know it is."

"It's out of my hands," Ward said. "Keep out of it. Let the law take its course."

Ward drew a knife, the blade flashing in the sunlight. He stepped toward Jellick, intending to cut him loose.

Rim said, "Maybe you won't be so anxious when I tell you what we found him trying to do to your sister."

Ward's face darkened and he shot a glance at Jellick, sweating up on the barrel. Then he looked around at Rim, his lips twisting. "You'll have to do better than that."

April cried, "But it's true, Eric!"

He ignored her and stood on tiptoe and started to saw the knife blade through the thongs that bound Jellick's wrists.

Ignoring his danger in the sudden rage that engulfed him, Rim sprang for Ward. He caught the man by an arm. Muttering an oath, Ward fell back, tried to slash Rim's face with the knife. But Rim drove him back against the bunkhouse wall. Ward came at him again, landing solidly on the ribs that Jellick's fists had battered so unmercifully in their fight. Rim fell back, nearly upsetting the barrel. There was a gasp from the men, a strange animal-like cry from behind Jellick's gag.

Three men climbed Rim's back. They bore him to the ground, face down. A man kneeled on each arm. The third man held his legs.

Sheriff Dort warned, swinging his gun to cover the Anchor men in the yard, "I don't want to kill anybody, but I will if I have to. This is a legal posse. If one of 'em is even scratched Anchor is goin' to pay. There'll be dead men in this yard. Bolden, tell your men to drop their guns."

"All right, boys," Rim said. "We've got no choice—for now."

Marcy Stallart stepped around Ellamae, who still held her revolver. Ellamae, staring at her uncle on the ground, made no attempt to stop Marcy. And behind Marcy came a pale but resolute April.

As Rim was hauled to his feet, he saw Marcy shaking a fist under the sheriff's nose. "You're a bungler, Sheriff Dort. Can't you understand what Eric Ward is trying to do."

"I only know this, ma'am—"

"Sheriff, arrest Jellick," April Ward said breathlessly, crowding forward. "He's the only guilty man here."

"I got warrants," the sheriff said doggedly. "I only want Rim Bolden to come peaceable to town. Judge Mitchell is here now and Bolden's lucky he can have a trial tomorrow."

Allie Grindge said, "Rim, we like both you young fellas. You and Ward. But we ain't goin' to let that stand in our way. We'll listen to the facts, us that's on the jury."

"I can see that," Rim said coldly.

"You got nothin' to fear if you tell the truth," the saloonman persisted. "Now you come along, Rim. Damn it, the town will look like Fourth of July tonight and we're businessmen. We are doin' this posse work as a favor to the sheriff—"

"But no favor to me," Rim said, and felt of the dented buckle where a bullet had come so near to taking his life only a few short heartbeats ago.

"Rim, you come with us," Allie Grindge went on. "You'll git a fair trial."

"You make it sound as easy as taking a drink of your whisky," Rim said, his voice heavy with bitterness.

Marcy Stallart's mouth was a thin pale line across the lower part of her face. "Sheriff, I heard you mention a warrant for my husband."

"For murderin' his brother in Kansas."

"You can't take him now. He's been wounded." Marcy's lips trembled. "If you move him and he dies, it's your responsibility."

"If he dies," the sheriff said, "it might be better all around. If what Ward tells me is true. And I reckon it is."

Ellamae, standing by the kitchen door, had let the revolver sag in her right hand. She lifted her gaze from her uncle lying in the yard, and looked at Ward. "Tell me it's the truth, Ward. You were telling it big in town."

"It's the truth," Ward said. "Now let's get—"

Ellamae cut in, "I ought to hate my uncle enough as it is, throwing me out of his house because I had a kid. But if he killed my father I hope he dies slow and terrible."

Stallart twisted his shaggy head, looked back at his niece. "I tell you again. Your mother was a good woman. Your pa was no good. He took my first wife. He—the gun went off like I told you."

Eric Ward removed his hat and looked at Marcy Stallart who stood tall, her chin lifted. "I want you to know, Mrs. Stallart," Ward said, "that this isn't my doing. Jellick is the one who told of a crime committed back in Kansas. I only repeated in town the things he said."

Marcy only glared at him.

Rim felt more vulnerable than at any time in his life. With a man gripping each wrist and another behind him he felt helpless. His gun was gone. He had expected Meade Jellick to make some retort when Ward tried to shift the blame to him, for Marcy's benefit. But Jellick said nothing. He stood some distance away, his eyes sullen, rubbing the circulation back into his wrists. The severed thongs lay at his feet, beside the ropes that had bound his ankles.

Sheriff Dort had been arguing with Marcy and now he walked over to where Bert Stallart lay on the ground. He started to haul the rancher to his feet.

"Leave him alone," Marcy said crisply.

"Mrs. Stallart, I don't like this worth a damn," Sheriff Dort said, and sounded genuinely regretful. "But I got no choice. I'm sworn to uphold the law—"

"Law," Marcy said through her teeth. "My husband is telling the truth. I'll stake my life on it. He killed his brother accidentally in a fight over a gun. After that brother broke up his home—"

"I got nothing to do with that," Dort said. "I hear a jury voted him guilty. I—"

Rim, watching the sheriff and Marcy from a corner of his eye, noted that the attention of every man in the yard was riveted on them. A tenseness had thickened over the ranch The posse had one end of the yard blocked off. From behind him Rim could hear Ed Rule cursing as the cook managed to get a bandanna around the hole in his arm.

Rim eyed the man on his left. The man was gripping Rim's left wrist. The man's holstered gun was close, so very close. With a sudden wrenching of his body, Rim ripped his wrists free of his captors, lunged forward, breaking the hold of the man at his back who had him by the belt. He slammed into the man on his right, knocking the man down. Somebody shouted. The sheriff yelled a warning, but Rim was in a headlong dive toward the man on his left. His fingertips brushed the heel plates of the holstered gun, but that was all. Something crashed down on him.

He felt himself falling.

April was sobbing, "You've hurt him! You've hurt him!"

His hands were drawn behind his back and securely tied with strips of rawhide. His mind drifted into blackness, then into light. In and out, like a tide.

Then it seemed much later that he heard Bert Stallart's tired voice, "I can make it, Marcy. Don't worry about me none."

"I'll go with you," she said.

"You stay here, Marcy. Boys, help me into the wagon."

Then Rim was aware that he was in a jolting wagon and that Bert Stallart kept talking to him. But Rim couldn't make much sense out of what he said. He realized he lay in one of the Anchor wagons, the one with the high sideboards. There was loose hay on the bed under him. He heard other voices now and the sound of horses moving beside the wagon. His mind gradually cleared. He got an elbow under him, feeling the narrow leathers cutting into his wrists. Even this slight movement set up a terrible pounding in his skull.

Rim heard men arguing. He cocked his head, trying to hear. He had the feeling that if he tilted his head too far it would slide off his neck and go bouncing back along the dusty road they climbed.

The wagon halted. The driver sat with elbows on knees, holding the reins. Rim moved his head, staring up at the high seat. The man was Pete Prentiss. Rim could tell because he saw the dirty string across the back of the man's head that held the eyepatch in place.

The wagon moved again and Allie Grindge said peevishly, "Why can't we hurry it up, Sheriff? We're losing money by not being in town."

"We can't go no faster with this wagon," Sheriff Dort said irritably. "This whole business is makin' me sick to my stomach."

"Easy there, Dort," Rim heard Eric Ward say. "You've got your duty to perform."

Rim felt something nudge him and he looked around. Bert Stallart's eyes were open. He lay on his side. His wrists were manacled in front. "Turn your back to me, Rim," Stallart whispered.

A faint hope lifted in Rim. He looked around. He couldn't see anybody because the riders were in front of the wagon and at the side. The high sideboards hid them from view. Only Pete Prentiss, if he glanced around, could see what was going on. But Prentiss kept his eye on the team pulling the heavy wagon up the grade.

Rim felt Stallart's strong teeth begin to work on the leather thongs. Once Stallart's teeth pinched the skin and Rim winced. But he made no outcry. It was the least of his hurts, anyway. His head was pounding from being struck down. And his stomach seemed to be one large bruise from the bullet that had ricocheted off his belt buckle. The sky was darkening. He saw a flare of light through a crack in the sideboards as a man touched match to cold cigar.

The wagon halted again and there was more argument.

Then Sheriff Dort said tiredly, "All right. You boys got business in town. And some of you got families to tend to. You go on ahead. We'll be all right now. Can't move fast anyhow 'cause we might bust open Stallart's wounds. And I promised Mrs. Stallart we'd go easy."

"Got to save him for hangin'," the one-eyed Pete Prentiss said from the wagon seat.

There was the sound of more voices and Rim whispered, "Faster, Bert. For God's sake—"

He felt the leather thongs part. He lay very still, trying to hear what the men were saying out there. Then Allie Grindge said, "Let's go, boys. The sheriff can handle it."

Rim cried, "Allie, goddam it, don't leave us out here!"

He hoped fervently that Allie Grindge would push his horse up to the back of the wagon where the tailgate was down. Rim had it planned in his mind. He'd try and pull the saloonman from the saddle and at the same time grab his gun.

But Grindge rode up to the right side of the wagon. He stood up in the stirrups peering down through his spectacles. "It's all right, Rim. You got the sheriff to look out for you. And I do have a big night tonight. Lots of fellas in town—"

"Are a few dollars in the till worth a man's life, Allie?"

The sheriff came up then and said something to Grindge.

Eric Ward said, "Pete and Jellick and I can handle things. The rest of my boys go in with Grindge and the others. We'll see you in a couple of hours."

CHAPTER TWENTY-TWO

Rim lay quietly, hands behind his back so if any of them looked in they would think he was still tied. There were the sounds of a general exodus. Riders moved away from the wagon at a gallop. Silently Rim cursed Allie Grindge. Why hadn't Grindge come to the rear of the wagon where a man could get his hands on a weapon?

Then he heard Sheriff Dort say, "All right, we're alone now, Eric. What's this about a plan? It better be a good one."

"You know that you're in this pretty deep," Ward said smoothly. "We can say that you played along so that we could smash Anchor and get ourselves a herd to sell to your brother at Fort Slaughter."

"Just what in the hell are you gettin' at?"

"This. We've got Anchor right in our hands." Ward's voice shook slightly with excitement. "All we have to do now is reach out and take it."

"I see," and the sheriff's voice seemed to suddenly chill. "And what about the Anchor crew? You think they'll let you take the ranch?"

"You saw how they acted today. Hell, they didn't even put up a fight."

"That was because there were women in the yard," Sheriff Dort said. "Now you listen to me, Eric. I've had about enough of your dirty game—" The sheriff uttered a strangled cry. There was the sound of a falling body.

"Meade, you damned savage," Ward said shakily. "You used a knife on him."

"Better a gun?" Meade Jellick said, "and have the boys come roarin' back to see what the trouble is?"

Rim lay still, hardly daring to draw a deep breath. His arms hung loosely, completely without feeling.

For the first time since the war when they could see the glow of Sherman's campfires and they had no food or ammunition, Rim prayed. Dear God, he said silently, just give me the strength to do this one thing.

But he knew the odds. What chance did a man have? He felt the blood surging through the veins of his arms, bringing with it ten thousand needle pricks of pain.

Quietly Rim got to his knees, intending to grab Pete Prentiss by the back of the shirt and topple him from the wagon seat and get his gun.

There was a sudden sharp explosion behind him and he felt the lashing breath of a bullet stir the back of his shirt. And he thought, It's all over. This is the very end of everything.

But he saw to his surprise that Pete Prentiss had thrown his hands wide open. There was a small hole in the center of his back. Prentiss turned sideways, dropping the reins. His arms waving wildly, he fell, dropping from Rim's vision beyond the wagon sideboard. And in that moment the wagon lurched suddenly into motion.

Ward yelled, "Jellick, grab that team!"

There was shouting and the squeal of a horse in pain. Then Ward's sharp scream was a chilling sound. The sudden forward thrust of the wagon knocked Rim down on the jolting bed. Turning, he saw Stallart huddled against the sideboard, his eyes closed. Gripped in the hands manacled in front of him was a small ladies' revolver. A finger of smoke from the muzzle drifted against the spreading stain on Stallart's bandaged thigh.

It took Rim only a moment to grasp this. Then he seized the revolver, turning. He saw many things in the instant he stared back. The ground was rushing away from the careening wagon. He saw the high mountains, the trees bending in the spring wind that swept down from the Colorado plains. He saw something twisted on the ground twenty yards back. Pete Prentiss, one leg at a grotesque angle, a jutting bone like a broken finger showing from a rip in his pants. Beyond was the sheriff, kneeling as if in an attitude of prayer. And nearer to the bouncing lowered tailgate that clattered like a Gattling gun, he saw Eric Ward on his back, hands pressed down on his face.

Cutting through the dust that boiled up from the hoofs of the runaway team, came the giant Meade Jellick. His bandaged head was low over the neck of his thundering Morgan horse. There was a jet of orange-red flame from Jellick's hand. The bullet neatly carved a long splinter of wood from a sideboard near Rim's head. He felt the sting of splinters in his cheek. Bracing himself, he fired. But the small weapon was either inaccurate or the surging bed of the wagon threw off his aim. Jellick was getting closer. Close enough for Rim to see his eyes, see the flecks of saliva on the jaws of the big Morgan.

Another shot from Jellick's gun. Rim found himself crumpled against a sideboard. And for a moment he didn't know whether he was hit or whether the wagon, skidding now in a tight turn, had toppled him. He felt a sudden tremendous shock as one of the sideboards was ripped away. He saw the spokes of a splintered wheel arcing into the low branches of pines. He saw the gashing of bark on tree trunks as the wagon scraped its way into a grove of trees. Then it lurched, came to a jarring halt. Rim found himself on the ground.

Panicked, he rose. He couldn't see Jellick now, but he could hear him beyond the trees. The wagon was on its side a few feet away. Stallart lay near a shattered wheel. Through the trees he could see the team dragging the broken wagon tongue, just disappearing around a bend in the road.

Desperately Rim tried to get his mind working. He searched for the revolver that had been jarred loose by the fall. He thought he saw it in the brush. But it was only an old canteen. He reached to part some brush.

But his right hand refused to move at the frantic signal from his brain. And he saw the arm hanging loosely at his side, felt the warm spreading of his own blood along his wrist.

He heard Jellick's horse beyond the trees, heard Jellick on his feet now, pounding forward, searching. Then Rim saw something in the ruined wagon that gave him a faint hope. Wedged under the smashed-down seat was a rifle, evidently left there by Pete Prentiss.

Lurching through the trees he reached the wagon, saw one of the angle irons of the seat suddenly bend grotesquely under a ricochet that whipped high, sending down a shower of pine needles.

He could hear Jellick's labored breathing now back in the trees. He tugged on the rifle butt with his left hand. For one frozen moment the weapon refused to move from under the ruined seat. But then it was free in his hands. He fell aside as Jellick, rearing up like some wild beast in the shadowed grove, sent a shot into the wagon.

Keep calm, Rim thought as he fell. He had bragged that in four years of war he had learned calmness. With his useless right arm dangling, he rolled to his side. He clamped the butt of the rifle between his knees. His left hand worked the loading lever. Then, holding the rifle in his left hand like a revolver, he tried to get up.

But Jellick was on him. Jellick's weight flattened him to the ground.

And he realized then that in one hand Jellick carried a rope. Rim tried to struggle and Jellick, kneeling on the injured right arm brought a scream of pain to his lips. Jellick slapped the rifle out of his hands, got the noose around Rim's neck. Then Jellick was on his feet, hauling on the rope. The noose dug cruelly into Rim's throat, cutting off his wind.

Above the roaring in his head he heard Jellick shout, "Hang *me,* will you?"

Then Jellick was dragging him across the uneven ground. But Rim had managed to hook his left forefinger into the trigger guard of the rifle.

Suddenly he no longer moved and he saw Jellick hurling the coil of rope over a thick tree branch. Then Jellick heaved on the rope. Rim felt a splintering pain in his neck as the weight of his body pulled against the rope. He felt his tongue pop from his mouth. A redness momentarily masked his vision. But he got a knee under him, easing the strain. He came up with the rifle and Jellick seemed to notice for the first time that he held the weapon.

Jellick dropped the end of the rope, brought up his own belt gun. Rim felt the shock of the bullet that turned him sideways. As he fell he jerked on the rifle trigger. He saw the right side of Jellick's jaw disintegrate, saw exposed bone. Jellick went to his knees, still gripping the revolver. His eyes were glassy from shock.

Rim, half-fallen across the rifle, used the weight of his body to hold the weapon while he cocked it. Jellick was laboriously trying to lift the revolver as if it had suddenly been weighted by stone.

This time Rim aimed for the thickest part of the body. He didn't even hear the shot because of the roaring in his head. But he saw Jellick fall back. Jellick's legs were doubled up under him. Jellick didn't move—

Somehow Rim managed to get to his feet. He bent over Jellick. The man was dead. He thought in that moment how much the man had cost this country. Dragging the rifle he staggered to the wagon. Stallart was unconscious.

He was vaguely aware of the sound of hard-ridden horses bearing down from the direction of town, and also from Anchor Bar.

It was the Anchor bunch who arrived first. Ed Rule, one arm in a crude sling, was in the lead. When he saw Rim he yelled something and drew rein. Other Anchor men swung down. They were surrounding Rim, their guns drawn, when Allie Grindge and the bunch that had started for town, surged back.

"We heard shootin'," the saloonman said. Then he broke off when he saw the wrecked wagon and the bodies strewn in its path.

Rim sat down suddenly and waved his men aside so he could see Grindge and the others. "Thanks, Allie," he said thickly, "for playing Ward's dirty game."

"But I never—" Grindge broke off.

In the crowd were two of Ward's men, sent on ahead with the town bunch. Ward hadn't wanted any more witnesses than necessary. The two men were strangely quiet.

One of the Anchor men, bending over something down the road, said, "Ward's dead. Somethin' smashed his skull. Hoss, maybe, or a wagon wheel."

"Better take a look at the sheriff, somebody," another man yelled. "He's got a knife in him but he ain't dead."

It was all Rim remembered until he woke up in one of the bedrooms at Anchor. His right arm felt numb and he saw the bandage and felt the other bandage at his side.

Marcy stood looking down at him, her dark eyes wet. "Thank God you're conscious—"

"How long—since it happened?"

"Yesterday."

Rim tried to think. "How's Bert?"

"Doc Snider is with him. Bert will be all right. Doc would have been here sooner but he was delivering a baby."

Rim struggled up in the bed fell back. Marcy put an arm across his shoulders. He sank back to the pillows she piled behind him. "It's war now, Marcy," Rim said. "We've got to fight this thing to the end."

"One thing is straightened up at least," she said in a dead voice. "The sheriff told how he'd been taken in by Ward. He told of Jellick's treachery with the knife."

"Dort is still alive?"

She shook her dark head. "He died regretting that before he came here yesterday he wrote a letter to the sheriff at the town where Bert— where Bert was sentenced to hang. They'll be coming for him." She spread her hands, looked away.

It was an effort for Rim to swing his feet out of the bed. His head swam. Marcy protested when he tried to stand. He sank to the bed.

"Find out if Bert can be moved," he snapped. "If he can, I want another wagon. I want you and Bert to head south. Take Ed Rule with you. And ten men. Head for the border. Stay across the line at Paso until you hear from me."

"Bert can't run for the rest of his life—"

"You do what I say, Marcy. I'm running things now. Bert isn't going back to Kansas to hang for the accidental shooting of his brother."

"All these tears, this blood. Because of the greed of two men, Ward and Jellick. I hope they suffer, wherever they are."

"You do what I say, Marcy. Get that wagon. When they come from Kansas for Bert, I'll explain. If they won't listen, I'll sell out Anchor. I'll join you both in Mexico. We'll start a new Anchor down there."

She swallowed and lowered her eyes. "We owe you so much. And after what Bert has done to you—"

"He's evened it up. He saved my life. He shot Pete Prentiss. I couldn't have handled them all."

"He told me. It was Ellamae's gun."

Rim frowned. "Don't tell me Ellamae had a change of heart."

"I don't know," Marcy said, "and she didn't tell me before she left. All I know is that you were unconscious in the yard. Just before they put you and Bert into the wagon she beat at him with her fists. Calling him the murderer of her father. I guess she slipped the gun under his shirt."

"Maybe there's some good in her after all. Maybe—"

"Perhaps it was something Bert told her in the yard, I don't know. Something that stirred her memory. Something her mother told her when she was a little girl. Something she overheard. About her father. Anyway, before she left she said it was possible that what Bert said was true. That her father was the sort of person who could break up a man's home."

"She's come to her senses at last."

Marcy shook her head. "People don't change that quickly. She's going to Tucson. You haven't asked about Ward's sister," she added.

Rim stared down at the clean white bandage on his arm. He felt sick, and knew that a fever was climbing through him. "She'll blame me for her brother's death."

"She shouldn't. She knows the truth about Ward now. She heard it from those who were there when the sheriff talked. It's a great shock to her. She wants to go back to St. Louis. At least that's what she said last night."

"Well, I suppose a gentle girl like that has no place in this rough country."

"I was a gentle girl once, Rim. This country isn't too rough for me. I almost gave up, but not quite. Thanks to you."

The door opened and Doc Snider came in, looking tired. He sat down on the edge of the bed, put a hand against Rim's forehead. "You've got no business sitting up."

"I've told Marcy what's to be done," Rim said.

Marcy shook her head. "I can't leave now. You'll need somebody to nurse you—"

Doc Snider fingered his graying goatee. "There's a Miss Ward in LaVentana. Maybe you could get her to come out here, Marcy."

"I thought she was going back to St. Louis," Rim said.

"You know how the stage schedules are around here Rim," the doctor said. "Chances are she hasn't left yet. I happen to know she purposely missed the noon stage—"

Rim said, "I'll ride in."

Doc Snider snorted. "You'll stay in bed. Send a man in with a message. I have a feeling she's waiting for it."

ABOUT THE AUTHOR

Dudley Dean McGaughey (1906-1986) was a prolific author of western pulp fiction under many pseudonyms, including Dean Owen, Dudley Dean, Dean McCoy.

www.ingramcontent.com/pod-product-compliance
Lightning Source LLC
Chambersburg PA
CBHW022033170626
46808CB00003B/1173